Long Way Home

A Mangrove Island Novel, Book One

Neve Cottrell

Cover Design by: Cheeky Covers
Formatting by: Polgarus Studio

ISBN 978-0-9908516-0-8 (ebook)
ISBN 978-0-9908516-1-5 (print)

Sign up for my new releases via e-mail here
http://eepurl.com/Z64nv or on my website so you can find out about the next book as soon as it's available.

Website http://nevecottrell.com

Chapter One

Heathrow Airport was not where Alexis wanted to be two weeks before Christmas. As she wheeled her Louis Vuitton suitcases behind her, she failed to appreciate the festive decorations and smiling travelers. Instead, she scowled at the perky and chatty students who were undoubtedly pleased to be returning home for a few weeks of parental attention and a much-needed cash infusion. Alexis was grateful that her student days were far behind her.

She wore what she considered to be appropriate travel clothes, a crisp, navy blue suit with sensible heels. For her, suits were like armor that she donned before going into battle. They also boosted her efficiency because she didn't waste time thinking about what to wear in the mornings. Every minute counted when you billed clients in six-minute blocks. Alexis had a specific suit for each day of the working week and even the hangers were labeled and arranged by day. Since this was not a business trip, however, she'd only brought the suit on her back for the initial battle that, right now, she didn't want to contemplate.

Alexis stepped up to the first class counter with her American passport ready and was greeted by a plucky young airline representative.

"Good afternoon," the young woman said with a broad smile. "Would you like to place your bags on the scale, please?"

Alexis didn't return the smile. She placed her bags one after the other on the conveyer while the young woman busily typed Alexis's information into the system.

"And did you pack your bags yourself?"

"I'm a woman, aren't I?" Alexis drummed her nails impatiently on the counter.

The young woman smiled tolerantly. Sadly, she was accustomed to much worse behavior from some of her first class passengers.

"And did anyone ask you to transport any items for them?"

Alexis gave an exaggerated sigh. "Does anyone ever say yes?"

Although the young woman's smile had faded, she ignored Alexis's question and soldiered on with the customary questions. "Are you transporting any sharp objects?"

"Just my rapier wit."

"Indeed. And have your bags been left unattended at any time?"

"No."

The young woman gently exhaled, grateful for the simple answer. "You'll be in seat 3A today."

She handed over the ticket and Alexis snatched it out of her hand. Without so much as a thank you, Alexis stalked off.

"Enjoy your flight," the young woman called after her, her cheerful exterior fully restored.

Alexis strode through the long passages of the airport, her straight and steady gaze never wavering from the next few steps in front of her. Nothing caught her attention, not the man who tripped as she passed him. Not the crying family as they hugged goodbye. Alexis was the epitome of focused.

Once the flight was airborne, Alexis watched multiple episodes of a television show she'd never heard of. It was listed as a comedy, but Alexis didn't laugh once. During her meal, the neighboring passenger made an effort at conversation.

"Going to see family for Christmas?" the older gentleman asked her.

"Yes," she said curtly. She offered no details and she didn't ask about him. He quickly returned his attention to the small screen in front of him.

Even though her chair could recline and she had plenty of legroom, Alexis retained perfect posture for the duration of the flight. When the sound of a crying baby was heard from elsewhere on the plane, a few passengers exchanged sympathetic smiles. Alexis didn't smile. Instead, she placed in her ear buds and pretended not to hear.

At JFK Airport, Alexis endured the long wait in line at immigration before continuing on to her connecting flight to Sarasota. Even after the eight-hour leg, she looked poised and together. Good Kate Middleton-style hair. Fresh lipstick. Wrinkle-free clothes. To anyone who noticed her, Alexis seemed calm, cool and collected. The kind of person who would be handy in a crisis, not because she seemed compassionate, but because she didn't.

With the flick of his hand, the immigration officer ushered her up. Alexis stepped across the line and handed over her passport. He took a minute to page through it and looked up at her in mild surprise.

"Been a long time since you've been here."

"Yes, it has."

"Welcome home," he said pleasantly as he stamped her passport.

"We'll see."

Alexis took her passport and continued on to her connecting flight. Three more hours to Sarasota, then a ninety-minute drive to the marina. The trip was already exhausting and she hadn't interacted with family members yet.

The Sarasota flight seemed no longer than a wink. Alexis nodded off briefly, but couldn't get comfortable enough to truly relax. Not that she ever relaxed. Efforts at relaxation made her uncomfortable. It gave her too much time with her own thoughts.

Upon arrival, she followed the flow of traffic to the baggage claim area. After another lengthy wait, Alexis finally wheeled her large and small suitcases past all of the reuniting families and past the cab rank, to where a town car awaited her. The driver wordlessly opened the door for her and took her bags. She didn't thank him either; she'd lost her ability to be thankful eighteen months ago.

On the drive, Alexis watched the Florida scenery whiz by. It seemed more developed than she remembered. Strip malls and colorful signage dotted the landscape. Yes, she was certainly back on American soil.

The car eventually turned off an exit ramp with a sign for the marina and Alexis felt her stomach clench. Part of her wanted to ask the driver to turn around and take her back to the airport. She bit her lip and kept silent as he eased the car to the drop-off point. No more cars now. Mangrove Island was car-free and Alexis wondered whether it was part of the reason she'd decided to come here.

Despite the hour, the sun was bright and Alexis stepped out of the car wearing her oversized sunglasses while the driver brought around her bags. Unsmiling, she examined the marina, thinking it actually looked less downtrodden than she remembered it.

"Spending time with family for the holidays?" the driver asked.

"Yes."

"Good luck," he said and tipped his hat before returning to the car and driving off.

The water taxi was waiting to take her across Mangrove Pass to the island where she grew up and fled the moment she graduated from high school. When she told people she grew up on an island off the Florida coast, most of them wondered why she would ever leave. From Alexis's point of view, she could only remember years spent staring across the water, itching to get out. She'd felt claustrophobic on the island. Castaway Cove, the neighborhood where she grew up and where her parents still lived, seemed too confining. Alexis had never felt like she belonged there.

"You here on vacation?" asked the operator of the water taxi.

Alexis had barely registered his presence other than the fact that the boat was moving. "Sort of," she replied vaguely.

"Be careful, you might not want to leave," he said jovially.

"I doubt that," she said and tried to control the fine hairs whipping around her face in the wind.

"If you're looking for a night out, there's a great little place on the south end of the island. The wife and I like to go there on occasion."

Alexis asked, "What's the name?"

He glanced back at her over his shoulder. "The Blue Heron."

Alexis blinked back surprise. She hadn't thought of The Blue Heron in years. She'd passed it on bike rides to the southern end of the island many times, but there weren't many nights out in her family, for a meal or anything else. Tilly MacAdams cooked what her husband ate and everyone else fell in line.

"They have live music there a couple nights a week," the man said. "If you're on your own, it's a good place to meet people. Nice bar crowd."

Alexis snorted, but the man didn't hear her over the wind. Nice bar crowd sounded like an oxymoron to her.

"I'll take it under advisement," she replied. The dock came into view and Alexis felt her heart skip a beat. Not long now.

"Do you need a ride to your rental? I could call you a golf cart. I guess you know there are no cars on the island."

"I've made arrangements," she said.

"Then you're more organized than most of my customers," he said.

Alexis didn't doubt it. She prided herself on her organizational skills.

"Here we are," he said, pulling up to the dock. He helped her out first, then turned back to retrieve her luggage. "Hey Don." He waved to the man sitting in the bright blue golf cart with white shells painted on the side. "Guess that's your transport."

"It is." She took her bags and paid the man.

Don climbed out of the golf cart and came to assist her. "See ya, Marty."

The water taxi operator gave a backhanded wave before returning to the boat. Alexis climbed into the passenger seat. Since Mangrove Island was a car-free zone, most people got around on foot, bicycle, boat or golf cart. Even at thirty-five years old, Alexis still didn't drive a car. Life in big cities made certain of that.

"So what's your destination?" asked Don, lifting her luggage into the back of the cart. He wore a long-sleeved blue and white floral shirt, khaki shorts and sandals. Alexis wondered if he dressed like that to get tourists in the right frame of mind.

"Rumrunner Road," she answered and he gave her a sideways glance.

"Which number?"

"Three."

He whistled. "I thought you looked familiar. You're one of Tilly and Greg's girls, aren't you? The younger one."

The observation made her oddly uncomfortable. She'd been living in anonymity for so long, she'd forgotten what it was like to be recognized.

"Alexis," she said stiffly.

"Alexis," he repeated. "You went to school with my daughter, Charlotte."

Alexis didn't have strong memories of high school. She'd made new ones at every opportunity, shaking off the grains of island sand and moving on as quickly as possible. "What's the last name?"

He chuckled. "I'm pretty sure there was only one Charlotte back then. Collins was the name. She's Burke now."

Alexis feigned a smile. "Charlotte Collins, of course. How is she?" Alexis still didn't have a clue, but her island manners began to creep back into her essence involuntarily.

By the time the cart pulled up in front of her parents' house, the sunlight had faded. Alexis squinted to better examine the front. It looked the same as it had during her childhood; tidy and well-kept save the cartoon-colored Christmas lights and oversized plastic reindeer on the modest front lawn. An inflatable Santa completed the look. Alexis shook her head. Unfortunately, those garish decorations she remembered well.

Inside the house, Tilly MacAdams was busy in the kitchen, preparing a pot roast dinner for her husband just as she had a thousand times before. Greg MacAdams loved pot roast almost as much as meatloaf and chicken parmigiana, so they were staples in the MacAdams house. As Tilly was about to drop the carrots into the boiling pot of water, the sound of the doorbell rang out and carrots scattered across the countertops. Tilly chuckled to herself and left the carrots where they fell. She hurried to open the door to a very unexpected sight. Her younger daughter.

"Hello, Mom."

Tilly realized that her mouth was hanging open so she snapped it shut. "Jesus Christ," she whispered. Recovered from her momentary shock, she absently wiped her hands on her apron.

"No, it's Alexis, remember? You named me Alexis."

9

Tilly raised a bushy eyebrow. "Both been raised from the dead, apparently."

She gestured for her daughter to come in and Alexis stepped toward her, unsure whether to hug or kiss or neither. Tilly made the first move and gave her an awkward half-hug and feathery kiss on the cheek.

"My Lord, what will your father say? You could have called, you know."

"I've been here two seconds. Let's not march straight in with the guilt parade."

"I meant call to say that you were coming today, that's all. You have to admit, it's a bit of a shock."

Alexis took off her jacket and hung it on the hook in the hallway. She didn't need to look around. The jacket hung in exactly the same place as it had seventeen years ago.

Tilly looked at her hesitantly, not wanting to assume too much. "Are you here for Christmas?"

"I thought I might, if you don't mind. I have confidence that you haven't turned my room into a gym or a library."

"No, no. It's usually for when the boys stay over." She paused awkwardly. "Your nephews."

Alexis didn't react. Instead, she scanned the rooms of the house for signs of familiarity. She didn't need to look far.

"Even the Christmas tree is in the same spot," she commented.

"Well, where else would it go?"

Alexis gestured to her suitcases. "I'll get these out of your way. Smells like you've got a pot roast on your hands."

Tilly smiled ruefully. "You know your father. Dinner on the table when he gets home."

Alexis walked upstairs with the suitcases and passed two high school graduation photos, one of her and one of her older sister, Betsy. She only glanced at them out of the corner of her eye. No desire to meet them head on.

Alexis continued down the hallway to her childhood bedroom. Unsurprisingly, nothing in the room was hers. Winnie the Pooh characters adorned the walls. Denim blue bedding. For the nephews, *her* nephews. A simple wooden chest of drawers stood against the wall.

Alexis placed her small suitcase on the bed and unzipped it. She stared at the contents, all encased in clear, plastic bags and neatly labeled. Her eyes burned with fatigue and she abandoned her immediate plan to unpack. Instead, she rifled through her purse and fished out a black velvet ring box. She cupped the soft box protectively in her hand. Opening the bottom drawer of the dresser, she hid the box under a folded blanket. Next, she removed a folded red cloth from her suitcase and placed that beside the ring box. With great effort she closed the drawer and her fingers hovered in front of the handle for a moment longer, resisting the urge to reach back in and hold the items once more. Pulling herself together, Alexis stood up and quickly ran a brush through her hair before heading back downstairs.

In the kitchen, Tilly had dinner under control and was pouring the requisite pint of beer in anticipation of her husband's arrival when Alexis entered.

"Anything I can do?" she asked, trying not to gawk at the change in her mother's appearance since she last saw her. Her hair was streaked with grey and the lines on her forehead had deepened into a perpetual frown.

"Do you still know how to set the table or does your butler do that for you?"

"You know very well my butler is too busy supervising my chef to do that. I have a wench for chores."

Tilly handed her daughter a small stack of plates. "It appears I do, too."

Alexis turned to the table to set down the plates. "Are you going to warn Dad ahead of time?"

Tilly pulled cutlery from the drawer. "I should, really, because I haven't renewed his life insurance. Too costly at his age."

The sound of the front door made them both stop in their tracks. The women exchanged uneasy glances. Greg MacAdams' booming voice came through the entryway before he did. "Tilly, I am so hungry I could eat the ass off a skunk without any salt."

He appeared in the kitchen doorway, filling it completely with his height and breadth, and his gaze fell immediately upon Alexis. His dark hair was thinner than she remembered and he'd gained weight around the middle. She easily read the range of emotions in his clear, blue eyes. First shock, followed quickly by anger, and then something akin to relief.

Alexis found her voice. "Hi, Dad."

"Your yacht must've sunk. Do you know you've washed up on Mangrove Island?" He examined her from head to toe. "You're too thin for a woman your age. Do they not let you stop working long enough to eat at that big law firm?"

"Depends on whether I've hit my billable hours that day."

Tilly brought his beer to the table and Greg moved to kiss his wife's cheek. He sat down at the head of the table while Tilly and Alexis brought over the food.

His eyes still on his daughter, Greg gestured to a chair. "Well, sit down. You clearly need dinner."

Alexis sat down dutifully. Tilly removed her apron and joined them.

Tilly's brow wrinkled. "I should've called Betsy."

"I'm sure Alexis will make time to see her sister." Greg turned his attention to his daughter. "So why does work need you in Florida? Some big company coming to wipe out a mom-and-pop store?"

"I'm not here on business."

Although Greg didn't comment, Alexis could tell he was surprised.

"I just thought I would spend the holidays here," she continued.

Greg chuckled. "What are we, the Ghosts of Christmas Past?"

Tilly tapped her husband's leg under the table and he

grunted in response. Alexis took it in stride. She hadn't expected a welcome mat.

Greg tried again. "Nice of them to unlock your chains for that long. Lucky you. Must've made them a lot of money this year."

Alexis changed the subject. She didn't want to talk about her job. "I'd like to see these nephews of mine." She took a small portion of carrots without any pot roast and passed the serving dish back to her mother. The small act didn't escape Tilly's notice.

"I should think so," Greg said. "They won't even know you."

"Greg." Tilly used her warning tone that Alexis knew so well. "Alexis said she'd like to see them."

"That's one of the reasons I'm here," Alexis said carefully.

Her parents fought the urge to ask about the other reasons. They rightly sensed that Alexis wasn't ready to tell.

"Do you not like pot roast anymore?" Tilly asked, unable to hold her tongue.

"I never liked pot roast."

"Who doesn't like pot roast?" Greg thundered. "Too working class for you?"

"I don't eat red meat anymore," Alexis said.

"No cheeseburgers?" Tilly asked, her brown eyes wide.

"No. Can't say I miss them either."

Tilly scratched her head. "Well, that will make planning Christmas meals challenging."

"You eat cheeseburgers for Christmas now?"

"Well, no," Tilly admitted. "We do a nice roast beef. It's a wonderful recipe from one of my magazines."

"I'm happy with a good salad," Alexis said, "so no need to make a fuss."

"Nobody's making a fuss," Greg interjected, quick to his wife's defense.

"More carrots?" Tilly asked her husband.

Greg held up his plate so his wife could drop another heap of carrots onto it. Alexis chewed slowly, trying to figure out how she could survive this visit and retain her sanity.

After dinner, Tilly and Alexis cleaned up while Greg retired to the family room to watch a football game. It didn't matter which game or team. If it was football, it was on. Nothing new there.

Alexis washed dishes while Tilly dried.

"You probably have a dishwasher now," Tilly said.

"I don't use it often."

"Do you use it to store pots and pans?" she asked. "I've seen that on TV. People in cities with limited storage."

"I don't use it for storage." Alexis wasn't a fan of clutter.

"I'll give Betsy a call and you can go see them tomorrow. I work until three, but it's her day off. Did you know she owns her own hair salon now?"

"No, I didn't. That's great."

"She's worked real hard."

Unlike me, right? Alexis thought bitterly. Her parents had always treated her accomplishments as less impressive than Betsy's.

"Are you still working for Morris?" she asked, changing the subject.

"Oh, yes. I've had to do a lot of computer training these last few years. Everything is computerized nowadays. Morris still insists on dictation, though. And he never answers his own phone."

"Some people don't like change."

"He thinks it's a real hoot that my daughter joined his ranks."

"I'll bet." Alexis snickered, remembering Morris and his orange and green striped ties and suspenders. Morris was a solo lawyer, one of the few on the island, who took any case that walked through his creaky door. Even as a child, Alexis detested his threadbare carpet and dusty shelves. As far as she was concerned, he did nothing to inspire a future generation of lawyers. Rather, he served as a red, flashing warning sign.

"Dad looks a bit beat up," she said in a low voice. "How's his health?"

Tilly shook her head dismissively. "Nothing wrong with that one. Outdoor living takes its toll on your beauty is all."

"Is he talking about retirement at all? I mean, at some point it's just unsafe for a man his age to do a job like that."

Tilly chortled. "Your father has been a maintenance

technician from the time he left school. He won't know how to do anything else."

"You could retire together. Do some traveling. There must be somewhere you'd like to go besides your own backyard."

"I think you'll find that Dorothy Gale learns a valuable lesson when she strays from hers."

"Wizard of Oz aside," Alexis huffed, "there's something to be said for getting away from it all."

"That's why people come here," Tilly reminded her.

"But don't you get sick of it?"

Tilly stopped drying dishes and gave Alexis a pointed look. "We don't all have a strong urge to run away from our lives, Alexis."

Alexis longed to say something in her defense, but decided to fight her natural instinct and keep her mouth shut. Instead, she resumed washing dishes with vigor. After all, she was here to reconnect, not to bicker.

"I'm still on London time," she said, stifling a yawn.

"No one will object if you turn in early," her mother said.

Alexis was unsure whether to take the comment as a slight. Despite the air of hostility, she chose not to. "Okay, then. I'll see you in the morning."

"I'll finish up here. Goodnight, Alexis."

She poked her head into the family room to say goodnight to her father.

"Already?" he asked, without taking his eyes off the television.

"I'm exhausted," she said. "We'll have plenty of time to catch up."

"If you say so." He yelled in response to something happening on the screen.

Alexis never had much interest in American football, even though she had grown up surrounded by rabid fans. In her adult life, she'd been surrounded by rabid fans of English football. She'd traded one irrational group of people for another and she didn't feel a part of either one. Sports never held much interest for her unless she was the one playing and she hadn't been part of a team since high school.

Alexis moved her suitcase to the floor and changed into her Natori satin pajama set. She barely had the energy to wash her face and brush her teeth before sliding beneath the sheets. She wondered what the partners at her firm would think if they could see her now, draped in denim bedding and Winnie the Pooh sheets.

Despite her fatigue, she stared into the darkness, unable to close her eyes. She tried to conjure up the memory of what it felt like to sleep in this room, night after night. The only thing she could remember was not wanting to sleep in this room one night longer than she had to. Mangrove Island hadn't fit into her grand plans. And now she was back, voluntarily. She pinched her arm to make sure the moment was real and winced as she felt the squeeze of skin. Alexis had done a lot of pinching these past eighteen months. Most people pinched themselves in happy disbelief. Not Alexis.

When she finally gave herself over to sleep, it was a restless night full of position changes and clock glances. She awoke still exhausted. Although she blamed the time zone change, deep down, she knew that this trip would be much more difficult than she had anticipated. How could she expect to turn up unannounced after all this time and not get questioned by her family? Of course they'd be curious about her life. She thought she'd mentally prepared herself, but she recognized now that her efforts had been minimal to non-existent.

Alexis remained in bed until she heard the sound of the front door opening and closing. Her father going to work. Must be six o'clock. She swung her legs over the side of the bed, cursing the jet lag, and urged herself forward. She padded down the hall to the shower. She wanted to be refreshed, cleaned, absolved. Sadly, she wanted more than a simple shower was able to give.

Chapter Two

By the time Alexis came downstairs, fully dressed and hair blown out, the house was empty. A small stack of pancakes waited for her on the counter, covered with a paper towel. She put the plate in the microwave and scoured around for a coffee mug. Since she was generally a healthy eater, she'd tried to be one of those people who started the day with hot water and lemon or a green tea, but she couldn't manage it. She liked her coffee the way she liked her whiskey, the stronger the better. London was a great place to indulge that need for a caffeine perk. It wasn't quite Paris, but the people there certainly liked their coffee.

She was relieved to see coffee still left in the pot. It wasn't as though her parents knew she was a coffee drinker. They didn't know anything about her adult habits. It seemed odd, yet there were so many other things they didn't know. Coffee seemed the least of it.

Alexis plucked a note from the kitchen table. Betsy's address. Within walking distance, she noted wryly. Betsy wasn't foolish enough to stray from her fan base.

She chewed her pancakes slowly, savoring each bite. It had been years since she'd enjoyed American pancakes. English pancakes tended to be thinner and less sweet. Alexis eventually gave them up completely after deciding that the bland taste wasn't worth the calories.

She sipped her coffee and wandered into the family room. She saw herself as a child on the same brown sofa, sipping hot cocoa and watching Christmas specials. She'd loved Rankin and Bass and Charlie Brown. For her, they'd brought a sense of magic. She wondered if they still played shows like that during the holidays. She hoped so.

After lingering by the front window, Alexis knew it was time to drop in on her big sister. As much as she wanted to, Alexis couldn't put it off any longer.

On the plus side, it was a relief not to wrap up warm and brave the damp, cold wind. Although she despised English weather, walking was still her way of life in London just as it had been on the island. Even when taking the Tube, she ended up walking blocks at either end of the journey.

She recognized the name of Betsy's street, although she couldn't recall which of her friends had lived there. No one she was in touch with. Then again, Alexis hadn't been in touch with anyone. She didn't belong to Facebook or Instagram or any of the other sites that involved reaching out to people you didn't actually see anymore. Alexis detested the whole concept.

Ahead of her, a little girl in a light blue jacket busily drew with colored chalk on the empty street.

"Hi," the girl called with a wave.

Alexis turned away from her, unwilling to give her attention. It took ten minutes to walk to Betsy's. She gave the house a cursory glance, all red bricks and cheap white trim. It was the future that Alexis had been desperate to avoid.

She rang the doorbell and immediately heard voices spring to life on the other side of the door. The door flew open and there stood Betsy or, at least, a version of Betsy. This girl was a woman, as well as a good forty pounds more than the sister Alexis had left behind. Her brown hair was the same shade as Alexis's, but the cut was short and spiky.

"Well, well. An early frost," said Betsy, folding her arms across her ample chest.

"Wow, let's do the time warp again," said Alexis, giving her sister the once-over. "How many washes can one outfit endure in a lifetime?" Betsy's fashion sense hadn't changed much at all; she still sported all black attire with loud, chunky jewelry.

"Do you seriously think I could fit in my clothes from when I was twenty?" Betsy asked incredulously. "You've heard about my three kids, right?"

"Only three? I expected a village."

Betsy's brown eyes narrowed. "How many hard-working small businesses have you put to death since I last saw you?"

"How many innocent beads had to die to make that necklace?" Alexis sniped.

"Better beads than children in sweatshops," Betsy remarked, eyeing Alexis's designer duds. She unfolded her arms, indicating a ceasefire. "So are you coming in or do I need to invite you?"

When she turned to lead Alexis into the house, Alexis spied a rose tattoo on the nape of her neck. She suspected there were a few more of those in less obvious places. As Alexis stepped inside, her attention immediately shifted to the home's interior. She nearly laughed out loud at the country style décor, complete with wooden chickens on the wall and red gingham curtains. No doubt Betsy had left the previous owner's style intact.

"Don't even mention the chickens," Betsy snapped, reading her sister's mind. "I haven't gotten around to redecorating."

"I don't think black walls would really work in here anyway," Alexis said, remembering Betsy's teenaged experiment with design.

A small boy appeared at the bottom of the stairs, clad in Star Wars pajamas. His hair was so light that it appeared almost white, and had the effect of making his brown eyes look even darker.

"Owen, this is your Aunt Alexis. You be polite, okay? No weird questions."

"Hi," said Alexis.

"My aunt's name is Kelly," Owen said.

"Well, this is your other aunt. Kelly is Daddy's sister and this is mine."

"Why haven't I met her before?" he asked.

Betsy gave him a pointed look to indicate that the question was off-limits. Owen nodded silently with his large, solemn eyes. His gaze flickered to the mysterious aunt and back to his mother.

"Why didn't you hug her?" Owen asked.

Betsy looked taken aback. "I did."

"No, you didn't. You sounded angry with each other and then she came in. No hugs."

"Your mom was surprised to see me is all," Alexis jumped in. For Owen's sake, she gave Betsy a friendly pat on the back.

"That's just our way of communicating, honey," Betsy explained. "Like when you and Brian fight."

"I don't fight with Brian. He fights with me."

"This is Owen, my youngest," Betsy said.

"I'm four," he told Alexis proudly.

"The other two are at school," added Betsy.

"When do they finish for Christmas break?" asked Alexis.

"Too soon, if you ask me. I need to get on the ball before then. I'm so behind schedule."

"Joey's not on the island," Owen informed his aunt. "He goes to a special school on the mainland."

Alexis gave her sister a quizzical look.

"Joey is autistic," she explained. "The school is for autistic kids. He lives here, but he'll attend school there full-time until he's twenty-one."

"Is Joey the oldest?" asked Alexis.

Owen nodded. "Why don't you know that? Don't you

have e-mail? The island has internet, you know, even if it's too slow for some of my games." An idea occurred to him and his face lit up. "Do you live on a deserted island?"

"Unfortunately not," Alexis said.

His tiny mouth drooped in disappointment.

"Owen, why don't you bring Aunt Alexis into the family room and I'll get us something to drink?"

"I want milk with a lid and a straw."

"Please," Betsy reminded him.

"Pleeeease," Owen said with enthusiasm.

Alexis followed him into the family room. A Christmas tree stood in the corner trimmed with colorful wooden decorations. Alexis touched one of a gingerbread man.

"We used to have shiny ones," Owen said, "but Joey kept taking them down and breaking them. Not on purpose. He just likes shiny things."

"And what's Brian like?"

Owen scrunched up his face, thinking. "He's seven. He likes to win. Do you think Santa Claus dies like people do?"

The change in topic was so abrupt that Alexis thought she misheard him. "Sorry?"

"Santa Claus is a human, right? So do you think he dies? Because all humans die or don't you know that either?"

Betsy hustled in with a tray of drinks. She handed Owen his cup.

"Owen," she said sharply. "What did I tell you? You can't talk to just anybody about stuff like that. Not everyone is child-friendly." She turned to Alexis. "Don't mind him."

Although Alexis bristled at the child-friendly comment, she simply replied, "I don't mind."

Betsy changed the subject without regard for subtlety. "So are you still at a fancy pants law firm?"

"I tend to wear fancy skirts."

"Guess that doesn't leave time for much else," Betsy surmised. "Not that you ever wanted much else."

Alexis cocked an eyebrow. "I think it's fair to say I wanted more out of life than endless paperwork and clients who act like spoiled toddlers."

"Do you have kids?" Betsy's expression brightened momentarily, as though Alexis's willingness to reproduce would change everything between them.

"No, sorry, I don't have kids."

Betsy moved her gaze straight to Alexis's left hand and Alexis could tell exactly what her sister was thinking. No ring. Guess she's not marriage material either.

"What have you brought me to drink?" Alexis asked, hoping to shift topics.

"I hope you still like tea," said Betsy and handed her a cup.

"I do." She didn't mention her preference for coffee.

"Hard to avoid it, I guess, living in England."

"Where's England?" Owen asked.

Alexis glanced down at him. "A bigger island across the Atlantic Ocean."

Owen's eyes widened in amazement. "Wow, the

ocean."

"So how's Joe?" she asked Betsy. Joe and Betsy went to high school together so he wasn't completely unknown to Alexis.

"Busy. We're always busy. Joe finally joined the union a while back and that's been good for us."

"My dad's an electrician," Owen said proudly.

"She knows, sweetheart."

Owen crossed his arms over his chest. "I thought you said she didn't know us at all."

Betsy and Alexis shared an awkward silence.

"How old did you say you are, Owen?" Alexis asked.

"I'm four. I'll be five in August. Supposedly, that's not a good month to be born if you're a boy."

"Why?"

"Because you have to start school right after your birthday and most of the other boys will be bigger and play sports better."

Alexis glanced at Betsy for confirmation. "He's worried about sports?"

"I'm not," he interjected. "I don't like sports."

Alexis immediately warmed to him. "What do you like?"

"Space. Dinosaurs. All kinds of books, but I can't read yet."

"He goes to preschool on the days I work," Betsy said.

"They have story time. And lots of toys," Owen said brightly.

"Sounds like a great place," Alexis told him.

27

Betsy turned the conversation back to her sister. "So Mom says you're here for the holidays. No skiing in the Alps or yachting in France?"

"I'm not James Bond."

"Just as secretive though," Betsy mumbled, then more audibly. "I'll go get some muffins."

"I'm surprised you find time to bake."

"You can always find time for the important things," Betsy said, never failing to miss an opportunity to remind Alexis of her failures as a sister and MacAdams family member.

Betsy returned to the kitchen and Owen sat on the couch, his dark brown eyes fixated on Alexis. She smiled as he continued to stare at her without blinking.

"How do you know when you're dead?" he asked.

Alexis's job often required her to think on her feet, especially when dealing with clients, but she found herself completely unprepared for this four-year-old.

"Well, uh, I think that depends on your religious or philosophical viewpoint."

"What's yours?"

Alexis shifted from foot to foot. "Um, I think you don't know when you're dead. You die and your brain switches off and you're gone."

"Like a computer."

"Something like that."

"My mommy says you go to a place called haven."

"I think you mean Heaven."

"Why don't you think you go to Heaven?"

"I certainly like the idea," Alexis said quietly. "I hope your mom is right."

Owen leaped onto the floor and picked up a plastic T-Rex. "Do you wanna play dinosaurs? They're extinct, you know. That means they all died and there are none left. Not one single one!"

Betsy returned with muffins in a basket and paper plates. "Owen, Aunt Alexis doesn't want to play dinosaurs. She wants to have her muffin and then I'm sure she has important work to check on."

Alexis shook her head as she bit into her muffin. "You've gotten even better," she said, still chewing. "This is delicious."

"Mommy, she's talking with her mouth full."

"Don't worry about it, Owen."

"But it's against the rules."

"Aunt Alexis has her own rules." Betsy handed Owen his own, smaller muffin.

"I want my own rules too," he demanded.

"When you're older, you get to be in charge. Make your own decisions. That's one of the advantages of being a grown-up," said Alexis.

"Yes, that and all the responsibility that flows from those decisions," her sister added meaningfully. Alexis ignored the jibe; she figured she deserved it.

"Will you come to my play?" Owen abruptly asked.

Alexis looked to Betsy, her child translator, again.

"His preschool is run by the church and they're putting on a Christmas play. Owen has a speaking part."

"I'm a Wise Man," Owen said proudly.

"I'll bet you are," Alexis said.

"Don't feel obligated…" Betsy began.

"I would love to come," Alexis said truthfully. She was charmed by her nephew and wanted to show her support, no matter how uncomfortable she felt.

Owen smiled happily and sang to himself as he chewed his muffin.

"Great," Betsy said and Alexis could tell she was pleased.

"So three boys, your own salon, Joe's in the union. Anything else I should know to be all caught up?" Alexis asked.

"If I didn't have little pitchers with big ears, I'd give you the local gossip."

"Another time," Alexis said.

"Will there be another time?" asked Betsy, without her usual ire.

"I have it on good authority that there will be."

"When are you going back?"

"Sometime after the first," Alexis said vaguely and left it there. She had no desire to get into details.

Although Betsy generally erred on the side of brash and brutal, she took the hint. "Well, it was nice of you to come and see us. I'd like you to meet the rest of the family soon. And maybe you could come by the salon one day so I can show off my place."

"I may be in need of an eyebrow wax soon," Alexis said, tracing her finger over a perfectly sculpted eyebrow.

"I can think of better ways to cause you pain," Betsy joked. "So did Dad nearly lose his liver when you showed up?"

Alexis laughed. "They were both pretty shocked."

"You're so lucky. Nothing I do shocks them."

"Not even the tattoos," Alexis remarked.

Betsy waved her off. "Oh please. It takes more than body art to annoy them."

"No, I guess the things you do don't annoy them." Her smile soured.

"I want to live in Antarctica," Owen said.

"Do you like the cold?" asked Alexis.

"No, but I like that no one else lives there."

Alexis contemplated this. "A lonely, old soul, huh?"

"He also likes penguins," Betsy said.

"I love penguins," he declared, jumping up and waddling around the room.

"I've heard lesser reasons to move somewhere."

"I'll bet you have," Betsy said.

Alexis held her hand out to Owen. "It was a pleasure to meet you, Owen."

He gripped her hand and shook it. "Same here."

"I'll see you soon," Alexis promised. It was a promise she intended to keep.

That evening, Alexis joined her parents for dinner and shared the day's events. Alexis talked more than she ate, which didn't escape her mother's notice. In light of her daughter's previous declaration, she'd deliberately cooked chicken parmigiana instead of the beef lasagna she'd originally planned.

"You'll get to meet the other boys this weekend," her mother said. "They're very jealous that Owen met you first."

"What's Joey like?" she asked. She knew very little about autism and wasn't sure what to expect when she met him.

Her father stopped eating and Alexis immediately sensed this was not a welcome topic of conversation.

"He's a wonderful little boy," her mother told her. "A lot of work, but wonderful."

"It's a damn shame," her father grumbled.

"Now, Greg…"

"What a waste. The kid is built like a brick house. Would have made a helluva defensive tackle."

"Do the other boys understand that Joey is different?" asked Alexis.

"Of course, especially Owen. He's clever." Tilly chuckled. "Well, you met him."

"Too clever for his own good," Greg said.

Alexis bristled. "He's four. How can he be too clever for his own good?"

"Oh, I forget who I'm talking to here." Greg dug back into his dinner.

Alexis pushed back her chair. "Thanks for dinner, Mom. I'm going to head out for a bit, if you don't mind."

Greg eyed her. "Really? You're asking permission to run out the door? That's new."

Tilly glanced at her husband with a sigh. "It's fine, dear."

Alexis moved quickly through the hall to reclaim her jacket. She felt the familiar tightness in her chest and knew that she needed some time to decompress.

"She's got a helluva nerve," she heard her father say. A statement she'd heard many times as a child. Her expression went flat as she grabbed her handbag and escaped into the crisp, night air.

A short golf cart ride later, Alexis found herself heading toward the south end of the island, admiring the festive lights and welcoming wreaths that adorned the pretty houses in the Costa Azul neighborhood. She'd always liked Costa Azul. Unlike Castaway Cove, where she'd grown up, Costa Azul was blessed with the older, larger Spanish-style houses. The island had been settled by the Spanish in the late eighteenth century, with the southern end being favored by its inhabitants. As a result, Costa Azul and Flamingo Key had the lion's share of character properties.

The area was eerily familiar and yet completely foreign to her. She saw movement as she passed by the various windows, evidence of life carrying on within the four walls of those houses, and Alexis felt a sharp pang of jealousy. A small, inviting restaurant caught her attention. The Blue Heron. The recommendation from Marty, the water taxi operator, came back to her and she allowed herself to be enticed inside.

Chapter Three

The moment she stepped into the bar, Tyler saw her and his entire world went silent. He no longer heard the chatter of bar patrons or the crunching of ice in glasses. The background music faded away. Even the beating of his heart stilled.

It had been seventeen years since he'd last seen her, yet he recognized her instantly. She was as beautiful now as she'd been in high school. Her glossy, chocolate-colored hair was still shoulder-length and, although she was slightly fuller in the body now, Tyler thought the curves suited her. Tyler was not the kind of guy who objected to curves. Deep down, he was relieved. Alexis MacAdams had always been his ideal beauty, his artistic muse, and he couldn't bear to think of her any other way. Now he didn't have to.

Alexis stood in the foyer and surveyed the inside. It was modern but cozy. Dark wooden tables of varying shapes and sizes contrasted nicely with creamy white walls. Not too tropical, but not trying too hard to be urban. The interior was tastefully decorated for the holidays with a few small, white lights and holly sprigs. Alexis decided this place would do for a temporary escape. She bypassed the restaurant area and headed straight for the bar.

Dressed in a red, silk blouse and black trousers, she didn't exactly blend into the casual crowd of flip-flops and floral dresses. She chose a tall chair at the end of the bar, next to a cluster of women enjoying a night out on the island in the run up to Christmas. Judging by the way they were throwing back shots, she guessed they were from the mainland.

"I know you," Tyler said with an easy smile, moving to her end of the bar.

Alexis assumed it was a come-on. "Don't think so."

"Oh, but I do. Alexis MacAdams, valedictorian of Woodrow Wilson High School. Class of…"

Before he could remind her of her age, she jumped in. "Okay, I stand corrected. I'm sorry. I don't know your name."

"Ty Barnes. Former classmate."

Alexis studied him briefly, his well-defined build and sandy hair, and tried to trigger memories of high school. His eyes burned with an attractive intensity. Even in the dimly lit bar, his eyes were the bluest she'd ever seen. She was sure he wouldn't have had those biceps in high school. Arms like those belonged to a man, not a boy. She'd worked hard to keep the past buried, though, and knew it was unlikely she'd churn up a name to go with those incredible blue eyes.

"I'm really sorry," she said with a small shake of her head.

"No worries. I mean, I haven't seen you since we graduated. You look amazing." He knew he should probably reel in his enthusiasm, but he couldn't help himself. He was still suffering from the shock of seeing her again.

"Thank you. I'll just say you haven't changed a bit and call it even."

"Ah, but I have. More meat on the bones. I was so thin in high school, I was practically invisible." He chuckled. "Apparently, I was invisible."

Despite her bleak mood, Alexis found herself warming to him. "Don't take it personally. I don't remember much from high school, except that I was desperate to leave. It seems like another lifetime."

"Join Facebook. Everybody's there and there's nowhere to hide. You can relive high school every day on your computer or phone or whatever device you're permanently attached to." He shook his head ruefully.

"If I'm on my computer, it's because I'm working," she said. "No distractions allowed."

He brightened. "Are you a writer? That's what you were into, wasn't it?"

Alexis registered disbelief. She wasn't used to being caught off-guard. Between Owen and this guy, she felt completely unsettled.

"I used to write poems," she admitted reluctantly. "How do you remember that? Hell, I barely remember."

"I played guitar. I guess I paid attention to the people who seemed to have similar interests. I still write and play music. That's how I started bartending, so I could stay flexible but pay the bills. Now I just enjoy doing both." He leaned casually against the bar and Alexis suspected he passed many an evening like this, chatting to pretty women. "How about you?"

"Well, I'm definitely not a poet."

He appeared so crestfallen that she almost felt sorry to disappoint him. "Oh, that's too bad. I was sure you'd do it. Fire in the belly and all."

Tyler paused to let the memory in. Even as a teenager, he'd admired her focus. She'd had a fiery determination that other girls lacked. He'd found her sexy as a teenager and he definitely found her sexy now.

"Fire in the belly?" she repeated.

"You were always on the go. Could never tell whether you were running toward something or away from it."

She smiled wryly. "A bit of both, I would say."

"So what do you do now?"

"I'm a whore," she announced after a dramatic pause.

Tyler raised an eyebrow, waiting for her to elaborate. He was confident that Alexis MacAdams had not turned to prostitution.

"Well, I screw people for money. Same thing."

He wagged a finger at her. "Ah, you must work for the government."

"Close. Greedy, fat cat lawyer at your service." She tilted her chin thoughtfully. "Actually, I'm not at your service, unless you own some multi-million dollar conglomerate that I'm not aware of."

Tyler leaned forward and rested his elbows on the bar. "You had me at whore."

Alexis's faint smile broadened, her first genuine smile in a long while, and Tyler was glad to see the scowl dissipate. God, he remembered that smile. It was all he could do not to lean that little bit further and close the gap between them.

"So do you actually tend bar or are you here for window dressing?"

He snapped back to reality, drawing himself up to his full six feet. "I'm sorry, I'm neglecting your alcohol-related needs. Let me guess," he said, assessing her. "Some kind of 'tini. Appletini?"

"Isn't that a risky way to ask for an order? Potentially insulting customers?"

"Am I wrong?" he asked, with a crooked smile.

"Whiskey, please."

He doubled over as if wounded. "Ouch. You've destroyed my average."

"I've heard that a lot in bars." The lie slid from her lips with ease. The truth was that Alexis rarely spent time in bars, even in her twenties when she was flush with cash and single. It suddenly dawned on her that, not only was he flirting with her, but she was flirting with him. In a bar. In her hometown. The moment felt surreal.

"No chaser?" he queried.

She cocked an eyebrow, challenging him. "I like to feel

the burn."

"An actual fire in the belly," he mused. "I like it. Is Jameson all right?"

"Perfect."

He poured her drink, added a drop of water, and slid it across the bar to her. "I have to admit, I'm relieved. I hate making those cocktails. Thankfully, most people on the island have simpler taste."

"I've never been a cocktail girl. Too sweet."

"Are you trying to tell me you're not sweet?" he teased.

Alexis tasted the whiskey. It burned through her core and warmed her from the inside out. "I may be a lot of things, but I don't think sweet has ever been on the list."

Tyler didn't doubt it. For him, her aloofness had been part of her charm. She may have been the girl in the next neighborhood, but she was far from the girl next door. He'd walked around in awe of her, which is probably why he'd never gathered the courage to ask her out. She hadn't been accessible, partly because she seemed to exist in her own reality, and partly because he'd built her up in his mind to mythic proportions. Back then, simply spotting Alexis from a distance had turned him on. Seeing her seated directly across from him now had Tyler's entire body humming.

"Listen, I can be finished in an hour. Do you want to hang around and take a walk after? Catch up. I'd love to hear about your life in the real world."

There was no way he was letting her walk out of the bar without trying to make an impression. He was older and wiser and had known enough women to realize that, for him, Alexis MacAdams remained the gold standard.

Alexis took a deep swig of her whiskey and, to her own amazement, found herself agreeing. It wasn't like her to participate in idle chit-chat, certainly not with a guy from high school she couldn't remember. On the other hand, the more hours she spent here were fewer hours she'd have to spend feeling uncomfortable in her parents' house. A win-win as far as she was concerned.

Under a moonless sky, Alexis and Tyler strolled through Costa Azul, deep in conversation. Talking to him was easy and pleasant, a far cry from the type of conversations Alexis had with her family.

"London sounds incredible," he told her. "I'd like to go someday."

"If you like New York, then you'd definitely like it. Parts of it, anyway. New York and London are soul sisters, I think."

"Then London is the much cooler, much older sister."

"I think New York would be happy as the hipper, younger sister," she said.

"Ha! As far as I can tell, New York's never happy about anything," Tyler joked, recalling a particular visit that involved an angry Mets fan and a dislocated jaw.

"It should sample a grim London winter and thank its lucky stars and stripes."

"You seem to like New York," he remarked. "Why did you move across the ocean? You could have been a three hour flight from your family instead of a transatlantic one."

Alexis shrugged. "Opportunity knocked and I answered." She didn't want to get into details, especially not with someone who never moved off the island. She doubted he would understand her need to escape.

"Do you like being a lawyer?" he asked. "I can't imagine myself at a desk all day. Too constraining." His broad shoulders twitched uncomfortably at the thought.

"It has its advantages," Alexis admitted.

"Like what, a fat paycheck to cover an inflated mortgage and a pricey foreign car?" Tyler scoffed. "No thanks, I live in paradise without signing my life away. The cost of living is decent. I own my home. I surf, kayak, and play music every chance I get. It's a damn good life."

"Don't you want to make it big, though? Is playing in bars on Mangrove Island enough for you?" Alexis asked.

"There was a time when I thought I wanted to be signed to a label, but times have changed. I don't need to play to make a living. I play because it's my passion and I'd do it whether I had two listeners or two million."

"Okay, then what about the limited dating pool? Haven't you dated every eligible female on the island by now?"

"What makes you think I'm in the dating pool?" he asked.

Alexis grew flushed. She assumed that he was single. "Aren't you?"

He took a brief moment to enjoy her discomfort.

"Between tending bar, playing music, and hanging out at the beach, meeting women isn't exactly a problem. Finding one I want to spend the rest of my life with, well, that's another story." A story that featured his eternal flame for her, although Tyler thought it best to keep that part to himself for now.

"I think it's great that you haven't settled," she said sincerely. "You've stayed true to yourself. Few people manage that."

"I guess you work such long hours, you probably don't have time to meet anyone."

"I definitely work long hours," she said, ignoring the latter part of his statement.

Her mood shifted and Tyler sensed that she was retreating. He desperately wanted to reel her back in. "So, in all your travels, have you been anywhere quite like here?" he asked.

"Ask me again in daylight," she said.

Alexis felt the light breeze tickle her neck and gazed up at the barely visible stars, blanketed by the dark sky. She had to admit, the island had a certain charm that she'd forgotten, or maybe never chose to acknowledge. She sighed deeply.

"Listen Ty, it's been great catching up, but I should get back. I'm staying with my parents and I feel like I have a curfew again."

Tyler didn't know what he'd said wrong, but he didn't dare object. "Okay. Well, I'm playing tomorrow night at a place called Gatsby's. I'd love it if you were there. Slap me with some of that urban truth and tell me how much I suck."

Alexis gave him a faint smile. "Maybe. I'll see."

They walked back in silence to where she'd parked her mother's golf cart.

"It's been a good night, despite my tips," he told her. "Thanks for catching up with me."

"It was fun," Alexis said with a note of mild surprise. She hadn't expected to actually enjoy her evening out. She figured she would sit at the bar and stare into a glass of whiskey until she was sure her parents were asleep. This was much better.

Tyler couldn't believe his good fortune. The girl he'd pined for in high school, the one he wrote soppy love songs about, his mythical muse, was back on Mangrove Island. He was so elated to see her again, to have the longest conversation with her that he'd ever had in his life, that her failure to remember him didn't faze him in the least.

"Have a good night, Ty," she said.

He longed to touch her before she climbed into the cart, a peck on the cheek, an arm squeeze, anything, but his nerve failed him. He realized that he still felt the way he felt about her in high school, that he'd never really stopped.

Alexis gave him a slight wave as she disappeared into the night. He stood there in the shadow of the street, wondering if, once again, he'd missed his chance.

Chapter Four

Alexis couldn't sleep...again. She rolled as much as the twin bed allowed, narrowly avoiding a tumble onto the floor. Spending the evening with Ty triggered memories from high school, of loneliness on the island and feeling apart from everyone else. She'd eventually moved to London thinking that a large, international city would offer the opportunity to find her place, her people. Instead, she'd found herself experiencing the same sense of isolation that she had growing up. Although she'd felt accepted in her law firm, it never felt quite right.

She stared at the magnolia ceiling, willing herself to sleep. As much as she tried to pretend otherwise, Ty Barnes unnerved her more than she cared to admit. She did her best to block out images of his strong jaw and the slight dimple in his right cheek. And those eyes. She didn't want to notice those things about him. And there had been definite flirting. It felt wrong. Alexis was disgusted with herself.

She threw back the covers and slid to the floor. Slowly,

she opened the bottom drawer of the dresser and pulled out the velvet box. She held the box tenderly for a moment before slowly opening it. A wedding ring sparkled inside. Fighting back tears, she slid the ring onto her finger, remembering how lovely it looked there.

Her wedding day seemed like only yesterday. Six and a half years ago Alexis had walked down the proverbial aisle as her husband-to-be awaited her, his trademark grin plastered across his face. Mark had looked unassumingly handsome in his classic tux. She'd worn a simple, elegant white dress with capped sleeves and a floral headpiece. No veil. About thirty people had attended, including Mark's parents, Donald and Moira Steamer. They were older than her parents by about five years. She'd had no desire to include her own family. At that point, she'd had very little contact with them and she knew they wouldn't travel all the way to England for a wedding. After all, they hadn't come to New York to visit her in college, or even when she graduated from law school and she'd still been in contact with them then. Granted, it had been sporadic and awkward contact, but contact all the same. They'd missed her college graduation because it was the same day as Betsy's wedding and no one seemed to feel that Alexis's presence was required so she, the first person in her family to attend college, gained a Bachelor's degree while Betsy gained a husband and a new last name.

For Alexis, the fact that her family was absent from her own wedding was a non-issue because they'd already been missing from her life for so long. It was difficult to explain to Mark's family; they expected a full-scale falling out that divided an otherwise close-knit family rather than a tale of gradual silence that began with weeks, grew into months, and eventually stretched into years.

Nevertheless, their wedding had been a wonderfully happy day. Alexis had hoped it would be the first of many more and, for a while, it had been.

Even in darkness, the ring sparkled as brightly as the day she received it and Alexis couldn't bear its beauty a second longer. She returned the ring to its box and snapped the lid shut, placing it back in the drawer. Then she retrieved a cell phone from the top drawer and dialed.

"You have one saved message," the automated voice told her.

Mark's voice. "Alexis, I do hope you're about finished. Not to be a nag, but I am sitting in an airport waiting for you on our anniversary. Greece awaits us. Come soon."

Alexis turned off the phone and quickly dropped it into the drawer as though it had burned her fingers. Leaning against the dresser, she took a steadying breath. She had promised herself that she wouldn't listen to the message again. She wanted to delete it so that she would stop tormenting herself, but she couldn't bear to part with the sound of his voice.

Unwilling to think anymore after such a long night, she climbed back into bed. Why did she think coming back to Mangrove Island would help her heal? Everywhere she turned, memories lurked. Maybe that was why she felt more relaxed when she was with Ty. She had no specific memories of him and the things he remembered about her didn't make her feel guilty or misunderstood. It was a welcome change. When she finally drifted off to sleep, she dreamed that a tsunami overpowered the island and washed away all evidence of its inhabitants except Alexis. She stood amidst the destruction, injured and terrified, and wondered how she got there.

The next morning, Tilly knocked once before entering the bedroom where Alexis still slept. Alexis stirred at the sound.

"Sorry, I didn't expect you to still be asleep. You were always such an early riser," Tilly commented.

Alexis opened her eyes and tried to focus. "Getting up," she mumbled.

"I didn't hear you come in last night. You must have been out late."

Alexis sat up, rubbing her eyes. "I ran into an old friend."

"Anyone I would know?"

"Probably not." Her parents had been even less interested in Mangrove Island's teenagers than Alexis had.

Tilly approached the bed cautiously, like Alexis was stricken with a highly contagious disease. "Your father has already eaten, but there are blueberry pancakes downstairs."

"Thanks, but I'm not hungry."

"Are they not your favorite anymore?"

"I'm not a child. I don't have favorite foods."

"Bacon and fried eggs are my favorite," Tilly sniffed.

"Well, blueberry pancakes aren't such a thing in England, Mom."

"Don't they have blueberries?" she asked innocently.

Alexis was too tired to mock. "Of course they do. It's just not a common breakfast. They tend to have more savory foods than sweet. Cooked breakfasts with black pudding, and bacon that requires a knife and fork."

Tilly walked over to the windows and pulled open the curtains. "Well, as much as I like a cooked breakfast, I don't know how you could live anywhere that doesn't have blueberry pancakes. It's un-American."

Alexis smirked but resisted pointing out the obvious.

"I'll leave you to your own devices then," Tilly said and hesitated before adding, "I thought you could help me make the Good Housekeeping holiday cake while you're here."

"You still do that?"

Tilly looked mildly surprised. "Why wouldn't I?" Shaking her head, she said, "What am I thinking? You don't bake. Too domestic for you. That's Betsy's domain."

Alexis refused to engage in an argument over her culinary skills. It didn't seem the right time. Instead, she said, "I had one of her muffins. It was delicious. She should have a bakery instead of a salon. That's what she used to talk about."

"The salon was the more sensible choice," Tilly said firmly. "People need to get haircuts. They don't need baked goods."

Alexis thought it was disappointing that her sister hadn't been able to combine her talent with her career, but she didn't argue.

Tilly sighed. "She does have a knack for baking, though. Such a shame she has those three boys."

Alexis's eyebrows drew together until her mother's meaning dawned on her. She gave an exasperated huff, which her mother duly ignored.

"She can certainly teach the boys how to bake," Alexis insisted. "I bet Owen would love it."

"Oh, Alexis. I don't know where you get your ideas. Joe would blow a gasket if he saw his son baking."

"Do you know how prehistoric that sounds?"

"We can't all be cosmopolitan." Tilly headed for the door. "I'll be downstairs for another half an hour if you need me. Then I'm going to work."

Alexis waited for her mother to leave the room before pulling the covers back over her head. She was not ready to face the day. In fact, she was beginning to regret her decision to come at all.

Chapter Five

Betsy wasted no time arranging a brunch at the weekend so that Alexis could meet the rest of her family. The house was in absolute chaos. Owen set up a puppet show in the corner of the family room, quietly practicing with his puppets while Joey stood in front of the Christmas tree periodically reaching out to touch the ornaments and then repeating to himself, "No touching." Joe, Betsy's burly husband, sat in his usual spot, the easy chair. Whether consciously or not, Betsy managed to marry a version of her father. No small wonder the two men were close.

Brian, the seven-year-old, bounced a ball around the room and peppered Alexis with Brian-centric questions.

"Do you know what I want for Christmas?" he asked in a rapid-fire clip. To Alexis, Brian seemed to be on a perpetual sugar high.

"No, I can't say that I do."

"Guess."

"She doesn't want to guess, Brian." Joe listened to his son with one ear and the television with the other.

"No, I'll guess." She pretended to think. "A pony."

Brian rolled his eyes. "Do I look like a girl to you?"

"Okay then. A GI Joe."

"What's a GI Joe?" He continued to bounce the ball, unwilling or unable to stop moving. "You suck at this."

"Brian!" Joe admonished him. "I told you before, don't talk like that."

"You talk like that," Brian spat back.

"And when you work and pay the bills, you can talk like that, too."

Brian remained unfazed by his father's rough demeanor, while Alexis cringed.

"Did you buy me a present?" Brian pressed his aunt.

"I haven't finished my shopping yet. What would you like?"

"A scooter, silver with black trim. No goofy characters."

Alexis digested this onslaught of information with a vague smile. "Noted."

"I asked Santa, but I don't know if he'll be able to bring it."

"Oh, why not?"

"My mom said sometimes Santa has so much stuff for other kids, he can't fit everything in his sleigh so he has to choose carefully."

Alexis nodded silently. Out of the corner of her eye, she noticed Joey pull an ornament off the tree.

"Daddy, Joey pulled another ornament off the tree." Brian ratted out his brother before Alexis could speak.

"No touching, Joey," Joe said firmly, but without raising his voice. He eased out of his chair and gently guided Joey away from the tree. Alexis was surprised to hear him speak to his son in clear, calm tones, not at all the volcano that Alexis expected.

"Joey, why don't you come over and talk to me?" Alexis suggested. "Brian was telling me about his wish list. What would you like from Santa?"

Looking blankly at his aunt, Joey dutifully sat beside Alexis on the floor.

"Elmo DVD," he said.

Alexis smiled, pleased that he answered her. "Do you like Elmo?"

"Yes."

"Elmo is for babies," Brian said.

"Brian! Be quiet," Joe scolded him.

"Do you like Elmo's voice?" asked Alexis.

"Yes," said Joey in his robotic tone.

"I don't really know much about Elmo. What color is he?"

"Red."

"You're pretty smart," Alexis told him.

Joey stared blankly ahead of him. Alexis wanted to give him some sort of affectionate pat, but instead she fumbled awkwardly.

"I'm ready to do my puppet show," Owen announced.

"Can it wait five minutes, O? I'm trying to watch the game." Joe didn't even turn to look at Owen. His eyes were fixed back on the television. She had a flashback to her own childhood, of trying to show her father a poem she'd written about starfish. Greg MacAdams had been similarly disinterested.

Alexis inched closer to the cardboard puppet theatre. "I'll watch," she offered.

"Yippee!" Owen hopped excitedly behind the curtain. A dinosaur puppet emerged from between the curtains. "Once upon a time, ages ago, dinosaurs ruled the earth. Some had feathers. Some ate meat. Some ate grass." Another dinosaur puppet popped into view. "I ate plants until a big meteor hit the earth and I died. Then all the dinosaurs died. Then there were mammoths and they died. Then there were humans and they all died. Then there was nothing. The end."

Owen proudly popped up from behind the theatre. Alexis clapped, quickly realizing that she was the only one. No one else paid him attention.

Just then Betsy appeared in the doorway to announce brunch. Everyone jumped up at once.

"The cinnamon roll is mine!" Brian yelled, expertly elbowing his brothers out of the way.

"I would think there's more than one," Alexis said, but the point fell on deaf ears.

They crowded around Betsy's small, round dining table where paper plates and plastic cutlery were set beside stacks of French toast, a plate of cinnamon rolls, bacon, sausages, and a pitcher of orange juice.

"I've got tea brewing," Betsy said as Alexis glanced around for a mug.

"Thanks." She wished she could pluck up the nerve to ask for coffee, but she knew it would only result in some barb about not knowing each other.

Alexis waited her turn as the men and boys loaded up their plates and disappeared back into the family room.

"Gee, nice of them to leave us a few crumbs," Betsy said wryly. "Good thing I made more." She carried more food to the table and stuffed a cinnamon roll between her teeth.

"I don't want to think about the calories I'm ingesting," Alexis said, piling her plate high with carbs and processed meat.

"God knows you can afford it," her mother said.

Somehow even her mother's compliments sounded like a putdown. Alexis was well aware that she'd lost a few pounds in the past year and a half, but she certainly wouldn't be considered skinny. Those days were long behind her. Looking at her mother and Betsy, however, she realized that they'd both put on quite a bit of weight since she last saw them and that probably made Alexis look particularly slim to them. Her gaze drifted to the plates full of pancakes and cinnamon rolls and wondered whether they ate like this all the time or whether it was a holiday treat. Either way, she had no interest in changing her relatively healthy eating habits just because she was back at her parents' house. After all, she had seventeen years of reprogramming under her belt.

"So have you been anywhere really exotic?" Betsy asked. "You always wanted to travel."

"The Maldives were really beautiful," Alexis said and immediately regretted it. She'd been to the Maldives on her honeymoon. It had been an amazing trip and she couldn't bear remembering it now.

"Where's that?" asked Betsy.

"A string of islands off the coast of India. Very private."

"Sounds like you," Betsy said and it took all of Alexis's willpower not to hurl a cinnamon roll at her sister's head.

"Did you go alone?" asked Tilly, clearly fishing for information. "That sounds dangerous to go somewhere so remote on your own. You always read about these solo women travelers getting raped or murdered."

Alexis rolled her eyes. "Mom, you don't read anything of the kind. I've never seen you read a newspaper in my life."

"I've seen it online," Tilly insisted.

"Well, you'll be relieved to know that I didn't go alone," Alexis replied and she caught the other two women exchange not-so-subtle glances. "How about you? Have you been anywhere?" She didn't expect the answer to be yes, but she was desperate to change the subject.

"You know your father doesn't like to travel," Tilly responded. "Joe's pretty much the same. Anyway, it would be difficult to travel with Joey."

Alexis noticed Betsy's slight irritation at her mother's mention of Joey. She suspected Betsy and Joe handled Joey's condition much better than her parents did.

"Joey probably wouldn't like being confined on an

airplane, but he wouldn't mind a car trip somewhere." Betsy took a long sip of her orange juice.

"Well, maybe this summer," Tilly said, picking up on Betsy's frustration. "Joey gets two weeks, doesn't he?"

"Joey's school goes all year round," Betsy explained to Alexis. "He gets one to two week breaks throughout the year."

"Have you talked about what you'll do when he's older?" Alexis asked. "Will he be able to live independently?"

Betsy shook her head. "Not Joey. Plenty of autistic people can, it depends on where they are on the spectrum. Joey's not going to be one of them, though."

Alexis didn't know what the appropriate response was for something like that. She longed to reach out and hug her sister, but it felt too unnatural.

"Oh, he'll be fine," Tilly interjected with a dismissive wave of her hand and Betsy shot her sister a hopeless look.

Alexis and Betsy's most sisterly moments had involved shared frustration with their parents. As much as she wanted to be helpful to her sister, though, she had no leg to stand on. If her mother wanted to live in denial, who was Alexis to drag her back to reality?

"Betsy," Joe's voice boomed from the family room. "How about some coffee?"

"Okay," Betsy called back. She pushed her chair back, but Alexis beat her to it.

"I'll make it," Alexis volunteered.

"You drink coffee?" Betsy asked.

"You make coffee?" Tilly added.

Alexis sucked in her breath as she retrieved a coffee filter from the cabinet and set to work. "You two act like I was some indolent slob who slurped tea all day and refused to help out around the house."

"That's not what I meant," Tilly said.

"Me neither," Betsy chimed in. "I just didn't know you drink coffee is all."

"It's true I didn't drink coffee in high school and I loved blueberry pancakes, but I hardly think people's eating and drinking habits stay exactly the same their whole lives."

Alexis hit the start button and returned to the table, relieved to get that minor detail off her chest. It certainly didn't bridge the gap of her seventeen-year absence, but it was a start.

When Alexis finally wrapped up her visit to Betsy's house, she was ready for a few hours of solitude before she ventured to Gatsby's. She'd decided to accept Ty's invitation while sitting in Betsy's kitchen, listening to her father complain about the current government. His complaints hadn't changed, just the names of the people at fault. The thought of sitting in her bedroom listening to her father yell at the television all night was unappealing, to say the least.

Alexis felt nervous about going to see Ty play. What if, after all his talk of passion and a good life, he was a terrible musician? What would she say? Alexis wasn't the best liar when it came to putting someone at ease. People skills were not her specialty. On the other hand, if he was terrible, he might look less attractive to her. That would be a bonus. Suddenly, a small part of her hoped that his musical talent would be nonexistent.

By the time Alexis arrived at Gatsby's, the bar was reasonably full without being too crowded. A few small tables housed couples while another handful of people stood around with drinks. She was relieved when no one showed a flash of recognition. She didn't want to engage in mindless conversation, catching up with people she didn't actually remember. She simply wanted to make good on her promise to Ty and get another breather from her parents.

By the time she scored a drink at the bar and located a seat at a bistro table, Ty was already on the makeshift stage, strumming away on an acoustic guitar. A smile escaped his lips when he noticed Alexis in the audience of rapt listeners. She gave a small smile in return, her stomach inadvertently performing acrobatic feats. She cast her eyes downward, unwilling to feel a connection. Instead, she listened.

His voice was smooth but sincere. To her, he sounded the way comfort food tasted. She'd forgotten how much she enjoyed listening to live music and Ty was surprisingly good. He wasn't exactly hard on the eyes, either. As much as she tried to resist noticing his finer points, Ty's hour on stage gave her ample opportunity to observe him when he wasn't making eye contact with her. Alexis found herself fixated on his biceps as they struggled against a tight-fitting, black t-shirt. She straightened up, regaining her composure. Since when was she the kind of woman who drooled over biceps? Mangrove Island was having a primitive effect on her. She gave her head a tiny shake and shifted her gaze back to his face. When he winked at her, she nearly spat out her drink.

"Aren't you a lucky lady," a voice commented and Alexis glanced up to see a petite waitress beside her. She wore her blonde hair pulled back in a tight, high ponytail and Alexis thought she looked like a cheerleader moonlighting as an adult.

"What makes you think that was for me?" Alexis asked, embarrassed by the attention.

"Well, it sure wasn't for me," she said wistfully. "I've made my move more times than I care to admit."

"We know each other from high school, so don't feel too disappointed."

"You went to Wilson?"

Alexis nodded. "Many moons ago. Ty and I graduated together."

The waitress sighed. "I wish I had gone to high school with Tyler. I would've scooped him up early."

"He's still scoopable from what I understand," Alexis said.

The waitress put a friendly hand on her shoulder. "Honey, if I believed that were true, I would sure as hell keep trying, but all I've seen is a string of girls who end up in tears when they realize they can't get their hooks in him. Heck, I'd settle for getting my hooks in him for a single night." She gestured toward Alexis's empty glass. "Can I get you a refill? What was it, a whiskey?"

Alexis handed her the glass. "It was, but I'm going to mix things up a bit. I'll have a beer. I've heard there's a microbrewery on the island now."

"Tropic Turtle. It's real good. I'll get you two."

Alexis wrinkled her nose. "One's probably enough for me."

"It's not for you," she said, nodding toward Ty as she sauntered away. "He's about to finish."

The waitress was right. By the time she returned to the bar, Ty finished his set as the crowd clapped and whooped appreciatively.

"Thank you," he said with a slight wave. He barely removed his guitar before making a beeline for Alexis. "You made it. I'm so glad." He slid into the seat across from her, eager to hear her reaction.

"You are really good," Alexis blurted out.

"You sound relieved."

She gave him a nervous smile. "I just didn't know what to expect. It's been a long time since I watched someone play."

"Too many billable hours?" he queried.

"Something like that," she said vaguely. "Your sound is very pure."

He looked pleased. "Pure, I like that. Thank you."

"So you wrote all those songs yourself?"

He nodded. "Told you, it's my passion."

"The crowd sure likes you."

"They're mostly family members." When her eye widened in surprise, he laughed. "Joking."

"The waitress definitely likes you," Alexis whispered as the petite girl arrived with two bottles of Tropic Turtle and two pilsner glasses.

"That was awesome, Tyler," the waitress said, placing his beer and glass down first. "You're so amazing."

"Thanks, Lily. How's school going?"

Lily put down Alexis's bottle and glass and smiled ruefully. "It's hard, but I'm doing it."

"Lily takes classes online," he explained. "Not easy to go to college if you don't want to leave here."

"Hospitality and hotel management," Lily offered. "I figure it'll come in handy if I stay on the island."

"Pink Palm could use some real competition," Tyler agreed.

"The Pink Palm Hotel?" Alexis queried. "That's still going?"

"Still does real good business," Lily said, "but word on the bay is that Roy Haskell hasn't been well since his wife died."

"That's too bad," Alexis said, her face clouding over.

"Some people don't recover from a thing like that," Lily continued.

Alexis's expression wasn't lost on Tyler. "Thanks for the drinks, Lily," Tyler said politely, letting her know it was time to move on.

"Let me know if you need anything," Lily said,

directing her offer to Tyler.

"Will do."

Tyler turned his full attention to the person he really wanted to talk to. "So how's your visit going?"

"I'm here in a bar, aren't I?" She sighed. "I'm kidding; it's not too bad. My parents are as expected. Same for my sister. Nephews are great, though. I highly recommend them."

"Yours?"

"Get your own." She sipped her beer. "I feel myself regressing, though. I'm hormonal. Prone to excessive amounts of sarcasm. Plus, my mom wants me to bake cakes with her."

"Did she dust off your Easy Bake Oven after all these years?"

"That was Betsy's. Pretty much everything was Betsy's."

"Ah, an old sibling rivalry rears its ugly head."

Alexis shook her head emphatically, rejecting his interpretation. "No, see, that's wrong. It wasn't a rivalry. We were too different to compete."

"Black sheep syndrome then?"

She shrugged. "Maybe. Probably." Alexis ran a finger thoughtfully around the rim of her glass. "I don't dwell on the dynamics. Anyway, it's the past."

"Really?" Tyler asked, his blue eyes crinkling at the corners. "Because it seems awfully present to me."

Alexis balked. She was used to brushing off her past. Easy to do in London where no one knew her. To her own surprise, she found herself wanting to open up to him. It had been a long time since she had a friend to listen to her. And the whiskey and beer combo certainly helped.

"Have you ever pushed something so far down that you forget you're still carrying the weight of it?" she asked.

"Then you must weigh a ton."

"Gee, thanks."

Tyler gave her a sympathetic smile. "I understand what you mean."

He placed a caring hand over hers and she felt a rush of warmth that she wished she hadn't. She didn't want to feel anything.

"Got any songs about love and loss in your repertoire?" she asked, instinctively moving her hand away.

"One or two," he said, trying not to flinch. "C'mon, Alexis. Unburden yourself. You've got two willing ears right here." And some other willing body parts as well, he was tempted to add.

Slowly, Alexis emptied her glass. "No. I wear my albatross with pride. It goes with everything."

Tyler refused to be deterred. It was enough that she came to see him play, even if he was an excuse to escape her family.

"Pride always comes before a fall," he said. Studying her now, he wondered whether that had already come to pass.

"Mr. Barnes," a man's voice boomed. Tyler broke into a broad grin and stood to shake the man's hand.

Alexis was grateful for the interruption. The

conversation had become more personal than she'd intended. She craned her neck to get a better look at the interloper.

"Glad you could make it," Tyler said politely. "Alexis, this is Caspian Warwick. He's one of my regulars, when he's on the island."

"Pleasure to meet you," she said. "Do I detect an accent?"

Caspian slid into the empty seat beside her. "Now that is a good ear. I like to think I've spent so much time here that I blend."

Alexis doubted very much that this gorgeous man had any intention of blending. Movie star good looks aside, he wore a hot pink collared shirt and navy blue checked shorts with leather sandals. His beach bum aspirational attire didn't wash with Alexis. He reeked of money and entitlement.

"Alexis has been living in London for the past decade and change," Tyler explained.

Caspian's face brightened. "How is The Big Smoke these days? Haven't been for ages."

"Grey and elegant, just as you left it, I'm sure."

"Tyler, I didn't know you had friends in London. You've never mentioned her." He clucked his tongue. "All those late night conversations at the Heron and nary a word, you naughty boy."

Alexis stepped to Tyler's defense. "We've only recently reconnected. He didn't even know I lived in London."

"Lived?" Caspian zeroed in on her use of the past tense.

"Live," Alexis corrected herself, her cheeks reddening.

Tyler gave her a quizzical look but said nothing.

"Well, I see a ridiculously well-proportioned young lady at the bar who seems desperate for my attention." He stood and gave Tyler a hard whack on the back. "Good to see you, mate. Cheers for the music. You're wasting your talents here." He dipped slightly toward Alexis. "Lovely to meet you, Alexis."

"And you," Alexis said politely. As soon as he was out of earshot, Alexis narrowed her eyes at Tyler. "Is he seriously a friend of yours? Where did you meet, at the yacht club?"

Tyler shrugged and smiled. "He's a character."

"You don't say."

"He spends a fair amount of money on the island when he's not sailing his yacht to bluer waters."

"Let me guess, St. Tropez?"

"One of many destinations."

"He's about as posh as they come." Alexis shook her head in disbelief. She'd had her fair share of dealings with members of English society through her firm and couldn't believe there was one lurking right here on Mangrove Island.

"He's fairly harmless unless you're a woman under the age of thirty, although rumor has it he's not very welcome in England. That's why he sails from place to place."

"Avoiding arrest?" Alexis was intrigued.

Tyler shook his head. "No, I think he served his time or had his day in court or whatever it was. A politician with a past."

"Aren't they all?" Alexis snorted.

Tyler polished off his beer. "Enough about the peerage, back to the steerage." He pointed to himself. "Based on what you heard tonight, would you be interested in seeing me play again? Because I can give you the calendar right now." He reached into his jeans pocket for his phone.

He wanted an excuse to see more of her. If he could gaze at her in the audience every time he played, it would be the best holiday season imaginable. He noticed the way Caspian had checked her out. Of course, Caspian checked out anything with breasts over an A cup, but he was justified in giving Alexis the once-over. She was breathtaking.

"Are you sure you're not trying to recruit me into your groupie set?" she eyed him suspiciously.

"I don't have groupies," he insisted.

"What about them?" asked Alexis, gesturing toward a trio of young women in the far corner of the room. She'd noticed them during the show, singing along to the lyrics. One of the women had her gaze fixed on them now. She quickly glanced away when Alexis caught her eye.

"Oh, you noticed them, huh?" Tyler said sheepishly. "They may turn up for a gig or two."

"Have you dated any of them?" Alexis asked out of curiosity. She hoped he didn't take it the wrong way. She didn't want him to think she was interested.

"Nope," Tyler replied firmly. "Too young for me."

Alexis coughed. "Too young? I didn't realize that was

an option for men."

Tyler took her reaction in stride. "I like a woman with a mind of her own. Girls like that don't have enough life experience and I'm not interested in having a lapdog."

"Well, now I know why you never became a rock star," she quipped.

"Isn't it past your curfew?" Tyler teased. "Wouldn't want your parents to send out a search party."

Alexis tried to ignore the push and pull of her emotions. Although she felt drawn to Ty, she didn't want to admit it, not to herself and certainly not to him. She wanted to use this trip to focus on mending fences as well as herself. Forge a new path. She did not want her new path to lead to a new man. She wasn't ready. Eighteen months wasn't enough time.

"Now that you mention it," Alexis said, "it probably is time to go."

Tyler fervently wished he could take back his last comment. "No, I'm kidding. It's early still."

"Is that why the bar is slowly hemorrhaging customers?"

He glanced around and realized that she was right. It was later than he thought. Only Caspian remained at the bar, charming the skirts off two dark-haired women while a few other people lingered over tables in the seating area. Even the groupies were heading out. One of them, Natasha, waved to Tyler as they left. He nodded politely but didn't return the gesture. He didn't want Alexis to think that he'd lied. Although he never actually dated any of them, he'd had a few sexual encounters with Natasha in the past. He wasn't interested in dating her, though, and that seemed fine with Natasha. Although she was pretty, she wasn't his type. His type was seated across from him and she was one-of-a-kind.

"Would you object if I walk you home?" he asked.

"It's not like it's a date," she said, a little too quickly.

"Of course not," he said. He knew he should ask more probing questions, but he didn't want to scare her away. Maybe his own feelings were clouding his judgment, but he sensed that she was attracted to him. Something was clearly holding her back, though.

"Anyway, I drove my mom's cart," she said, "so you don't need to walk me."

"So you'll come to another show?" he asked, trying not to sound too eager. "I tend to play more this time of year and in the summer. Mangrove Island is becoming quite the hot holiday destination."

"Good to know I'm on trend," Alexis said with a wry smile. "You can text me with details of your Mangrove Island holiday tour." She gave him her number and he deftly programmed it into his phone. She guessed hers wasn't the first number to be typed into his phone at a bar since he seemed to have no shortage of admirers.

He walked her outside to her lone cart. Everyone else had left or intended to walk home. It was a clear night and the stars shone brightly, drawing Alexis's eyes skyward.

"God, I forgot how pretty it could be," she breathed.

"I haven't," Tyler said. When she glanced at him, she

saw the flicker of desire in his deep, blue eyes.

"Thanks for tonight," she said and slid into the cart.

"My pleasure," he said and Alexis could hear in his voice that it truly was.

As Tyler watched her drive off, he wanted to kick himself. Way to play it cool, he chastised himself. On the other hand, he'd been waiting more than seventeen years to get her attention, so playing it cool didn't really seem like the right approach anyway.

His mind went back to her comment about London. Lived. Past tense. But she said she was only here to see family for the holidays. He knew something was up, but he needed to be patient. There was a skittishness to her now that he didn't remember from high school. Tyler knew there was a story there; he simply would wait until she was ready to tell it.

Alexis didn't ride straight back to Rumrunner Road. Instead, she drove to a nearby beach and sat in the cart, gazing up at the stars. The way she felt tonight upset her and she didn't want to go back to her parents' house brimming with emotions. She wanted to work through some of her feelings. Her therapist had recommended that Alexis allow herself to 'feel her feelings,' but Alexis hadn't been ready at the time. As she listened to the sound of the waves crashing against the shoreline, Alexis decided that she was ready to try.

She closed her eyes and let the soothing sound wash over her. The way she felt when she looked at Ty triggered strong memories of Mark. They seemed like polar opposites, though. Alexis had a hard time believing that she could be attracted to two such completely different men. She relaxed into the seat, allowing the memory of Mark to fill her.

She'd met him at work, of course, because that's where she spent the majority of her waking hours. Her desk had been in its normal state, strewn with books, files and empty coffee cups. As usual, she'd been reading through a contract and fighting off a headache. A knock at the door had interrupted her and she'd glanced up to see her boss.

"Hi, Hal. What's up?"

Hal Brookman was an older gentleman and a senior partner at her law firm. He was a familiar presence in her doorway, often stopping by to chat about world events or American pop culture. He was a huge Seinfeld fan, even though it had been off the air for years, and enjoyed quoting his favorite episodes. This particular day, Hal was accompanied by a man Alexis didn't recognize. He wore dark trousers, a cashmere sweater and black boots and, although stylish, he looked completely out of place in the firm's formal offices.

"So sorry to disturb, Alexis, but I would very much like you to meet Mark Steamer. Mark is in-house counsel for our new client, Biomyte."

Alexis stood up to shake his hand. "Alexis MacAdams, nice to meet you."

"Alexis is a key member of our team. Her work is impeccable."

"Thank you, Hal," said Alexis.

"You have the oddest English accent I've ever heard," Mark remarked.

Alexis opened her mouth to answer, but Hal cut her off. "Alexis hails from the States. She joined us from our New York office a few years ago. She is — oh, how would those Yanks put it — our resident ballbuster."

"I'll keep a close watch on my balls then." Mark blushed, realizing what he'd said.

Again, Alexis opened her mouth to speak, but Hal seemed to have a case of verbal diarrhea. "I'm afraid Britain hasn't quite won her over. She finds Wimbledon boring, won't touch Marmite and, if memory serves, she refused to listen to the Queen's speech at Christmas last year."

"Refusal to listen to the Queen's speech should be grounds for deportation, surely," Mark said.

Alexis smirked. Hal didn't realize Mark was mocking him.

"Hal's right," Alexis interjected. "Instead, I draped myself in the American flag and watched Top Gun while eating a hot dog and stroking my pistol."

Mark's smile broadened and Alexis's life as she knew it was over.

Chapter Six

Alexis didn't have to wait long to hear from Tyler. The next morning he texted her his show schedule, as well as a link to Lottie's Greenhouse with a question mark. Lottie's Greenhouse was a lovely garden center and landscaping company that hosted special events throughout the year. It was where she'd gone to see Santa as a child and where they'd go for their Christmas tree every year.

Sitting at the kitchen table nursing her second cup of coffee, she clicked the link to see whether he expected her to sit on Santa's lap. The link took her to a page about a Winter Wonderland skating rink available now through January second. Alexis bit her lip. A skating rink definitely seemed more like a date than two classmates catching up.

"You're up late again this morning," her mother's voice said from behind her.

"I am on vacation," Alexis said defensively.

"I'm not making a point about your work ethic, dear. When you were younger, you were always up before the sun."

"I think I used to hear Dad getting up," Alexis said, although it was true that she liked to wake up early. 'The early bird gets the worm' was her private mantra and it had served her well in law school when the library study cubicles were all taken hostage by nine o'clock.

"Well, you're sleeping through it now," her mother commented wryly. She walked to the counter to pour herself a cup of coffee. "Betsy called to see if you'd like to do some Christmas shopping with her."

"Today?"

She shrugged. "Seems so. I left her number there," she said, pointing to a piece of paper on the counter. "She also wants to confirm that you're going to Owen's Nativity play at the preschool. Apparently, he insisted on your attendance and she needs to tell them how many tickets."

"Clearly, he recognizes his core fan base. When is it again?"

"Tomorrow morning, assuming you'll still be here," Tilly said archly.

Alexis didn't take the bait. "I'll be here."

"Great, then you can let her know when you return her call." Tilly slurped her coffee. "So how does it feel being back here? Bored yet?"

Alexis rolled her eyes. "I'm not twelve. I don't get bored."

"You roll your eyes as well as any twelve-year-old."

Alexis felt her cheeks burn hot. She may have become a successful lawyer in a big London law firm, but one snide comment from her mother made her feel as small as a thumbnail. She wished she could extract all the hurt and misunderstandings from her family dynamics and start over. A clean slate. No preconceived notions. Her phone buzzed again. Another text from Tyler.

"Galleon at six followed by Lottie's," it read. "You in?"

Well, he certainly was persistent. She glanced at her mother's pursed lips and rigid face, a face that seemed so resistant to change, so unwilling to forgive.

"See you there," she typed back, and then she dialed her sister's number.

Alexis stood in the middle of a mobbed JCPenney, wondering what possessed her to accompany Betsy to a mall on the mainland right before Christmas. Too much holiday cheer and sisterly guilt rolled into one, no doubt.

They tried in vain to carry on a conversation while walking through the endless throng of people. The regrettable underbelly of Christmas. Christmas songs hurt her ears as young and old alike rudely jostled one another. Although Alexis was used to the hustle and bustle of a big city, in a place like this it aggravated her more. Probably because she expected better of them. Or maybe because she'd already spent enough time on the island to forget the reality of crowds.

"Brian is definitely the competitive one," Betsy was telling her as Alexis strained to listen. "The kid used to victory spike his baby bottle when he finished it. I was glad I wasn't breastfeeding anymore."

Alexis glanced around them in annoyance. "You must

be off the deep end wanting to come shopping this week."

She turned to look at her sister, but instead of annoyance, she saw a flicker of nostalgia in Betsy's brown eyes. "I don't get to the mainland for shopping very often. In case you haven't noticed, I'm a little booked up with three kids, a husband, and a salon." Her eyes turned toward two small children tugging on their mother's shirt. She was visibly relieved to be without children for the day. "Besides, this whole scene is sort of interesting."

Alexis bumped into a large man passing her in a hurry. Obstacles everywhere.

"Look, this might be some kind of sociological experiment to you, observing gorillas with credit cards in our midst, but it's giving me a migraine," Alexis huffed.

Betsy stopped walking and a woman stepped onto the backs of her shoes. The woman cast the sisters a dirty look before veering around them. "By all means, let's put our efficiency caps on. What is it you would like to accomplish here?"

"I'd like to find that scooter for Brian."

Betsy blanched. "The scooter? Why?"

"Oh, did you already buy it?" asked Alexis.

"No, it's expensive. And he's getting other presents."

"I don't mind buying it."

Alexis noticed Betsy's irritation but didn't understand it. Then Betsy shocked Alexis by dropping her bags right in the middle of the bustling crowd and pointing a finger at Alexis.

"Why are you here?"

Alexis blinked. "Because you invited me."

"No, I mean why are you on Mangrove Island? Why did you come back?"

Alexis's heart began beating harder. "Excuse me?"

"No one has the balls to ask the mighty Alexis why she has fallen so far from grace that she needs to flee Mount Olympus and join us mere mortals on our insignificant land mass." Betsy's angry hands flew to her hips. "Well, I do. So tell me Alexis, why are you really here? I'm finding it hard to believe it's because you missed us when you haven't been in touch in God knows how long."

Too exhausted from the pain-inducing environment to be reasonable, Alexis immediately shifted into bitch mode. "I'm surprised you could make a mythological reference. Where'd you learn about Mount Olympus? In a cartoon?"

"Still a smug little bitch. You haven't changed one iota."

"Changed from what? I've got news for you, Elizabeth," Alexis sneered, using her sister's much-hated given name, "the fact that you and the rest of the family labeled me an apple, doesn't make me an apple."

"Label you?" Betsy roared. "We didn't have to label you. You were all too happy to tell us who you were. Too good to cook, too good to sew, too damned good. I'm surprised your built-in hoi polloi alarm didn't go off when you set foot in this mall."

"If by cooking you mean tossing iceberg lettuce with string cheese and full fat mayo, then you're absolutely right. I am too good to do that."

Betsy crossed her arms. "Oh, come on. That was a one-time experiment and you know it."

"What are you really worked up about? The fact that I got out in the first place or the fact that I've returned successful?"

Betsy snorted. "You and I clearly have different definitions of success."

Alexis studied her older sister's flushed face and willed her own anger to dissolve. Taking a deep breath, Alexis drew enough strength to walk away from the argument before it escalated further.

"I'm going to get Brian that scooter," she said evenly. "I'll find my own way back to the island."

"Do me a favor," Betsy called after her. "Don't say the scooter's from you because when you disappear again, I don't want him to be reminded of you every freakin' time he rides it."

Betsy snatched up her bags and stalked off in the opposite direction.

Alexis seethed all the way through the shopping center. Hot, angry tears sprang from her eyes and she could barely see where she was going. Tired of fighting the crowds, she took refuge on a bench and closed her eyes to ease her pounding head.

She absolutely hated lashing out at her sister. Betsy was clearly harboring deep resentment and Alexis didn't really blame her. Her eyelids fluttered open and she took a moment to observe the shoppers more closely. She noticed a family of five trying to walk together despite the tide of people rushing around them.

"Single file line," she heard the father say. The three children scrambled into formation with the youngest at the front. Between that and the man's crew cut, Alexis guessed they were a military family.

"You look like you need a strong coffee," an elderly man said, setting himself down beside her. He rested his cane on the end of the bench.

"A strong drink," she agreed. "Not sure it should be coffee, though."

He chuckled. "A woman after my own heart." He took note of the absence of shopping bags. "Having trouble with gift ideas?"

Alexis shook her head. "Not the kind of problem that would stress me out."

The elderly man smiled kindly. "I always accompany my wife on her shopping trips. Helen, she's a real worrywart. What if little Jimmy is too old for this toy? What if I insult Janie with the size of the sweater I buy her?"

"Let me guess, it always turns out fine."

He leaned back against the bench and sighed. "Always. She gets herself all worked up for nothing."

"I'll bet you love being on the receiving end of that," she commented.

He scratched his chin. "You know what? That's my job. I love her and that's one of the ways I give her what she needs."

"You're very sweet."

"Hey, I didn't say it was a one-way street. She puts up with a lot of my nonsense, too. Nobody's perfect, not even close."

Alexis watched as two little girls skipped ahead of their mother, singing and holding hands as they went. She and Betsy had never been that close. In fact, she couldn't think of a single activity that they liked to do together. They didn't even listen to the same music. Alexis had plenty of memories of disagreements and aggravations, but not much else, yet Betsy seemed to have so much bitterness stored up over Alexis's voluntary alienation. Was it because she viewed the departure as a personal rejection or was it because Betsy actually wanted Alexis in her life? The former seemed more likely.

"Do you know where the nearest bus stop is, by any chance?" Alexis asked.

"Sure do. You got plans?"

"I do, actually. I need to get back to Mangrove Island to meet a friend."

"Mangrove Island?" he queried. "Such a nice place. My wife and I have spent time there over the years. Good fishing."

"You couldn't choose a better place for it."

"Don't I know it." He gave her directions to the nearest bus stop and Alexis thanked him before standing to leave.

"I just need to do a little shopping first," she said. "I came all this way, I don't want to leave empty-handed."

"Good luck," said the elderly man.

"Merry Christmas," she called over her shoulder as she hurried to find the much-desired scooter.

Her phone rang as she studied the directory and, when she saw Ty's number on the screen, an involuntary smile tugged at her cheeks.

"Hey, stranger," she answered.

"Wow, have you fled to Madison Square Garden?" he asked.

"Noisy, huh? It's a shopping center. Betsy keeps a car on the mainland for excursions so I went with her."

"Last minute Christmas shopping?"

"Can you blame me? I've been distracted by someone who keeps inviting me to spend time with him in the vain hope that I'll remember him from high school," she said.

"Ah, you've seen through my ruse. Is it working?" She could practically hear him grinning.

"Not yet. Listen, I hope I'm not late to dinner. Betsy and I had a fight and I'll need to grab a bus to the water taxi once I'm finished. I have no clue how long that takes, but I'm guessing long."

"A bus?" he echoed. "Don't do that. It'll take ages. I'll give my buddy Paul your number."

"Who's Paul?"

"Friend of mine who owns a car service. It'll be faster."

"Don't trouble yourself."

"Trouble? I'm being completely selfish here. I don't want you to miss our...evening out." He deliberately avoided the word 'date.'

She laughed. "Fine, you're a selfish bastard sending a

car for me."

"I'll see you tonight," he said.

"Thanks, Ty."

By the time she finished her shopping, her mood was elevated and she found herself whistling Christmas carols as she waited for Paul to show up outside the mall. A sleek black limousine pulled up to the curb, blocking her view. Alexis was still craning her neck for a car when a limo driver appeared in front of her.

"You must be Alexis," he said. "Tyler described you perfectly."

"Paul?" she queried.

He wasn't wearing the usual limo driver attire. In fact, he looked more like he stole the limo. Wearing ripped jeans and a faded Rolling Stones t-shirt, Paul did not exactly scream respectable chauffeur.

"Don't look so shocked," he said. "I'm not a chauffeur."

"Then why do you drive a limo?"

"I have a fleet of limos. It's kind of important when you own a limo company."

"Oh."

Paul held the back door open for her, but Alexis shook her head.

"Do you mind if I ride in the passenger seat up front? I'd feel foolish riding in the back."

"Be my guest," he said, closing the back door and opening the passenger side door instead.

She slid inside and admired the tan leather interior. It

was a beautiful limo. Paul hopped into the driver's seat and set off.

"So is this a busy time of year?" Alexis asked.

"Fairly. Corporate holiday parties and such."

"Well, I appreciate the ride."

"Anything for Tyler Barnes."

"How do you know him?" she asked.

"We met when we were about thirteen. Took guitar lessons together."

"Are you from Mangrove Island, too?" It wouldn't surprise Alexis to learn that Paul, too, had attended Wilson with her.

He shook his thick head of wavy, black hair. "He took lessons in Fort Myers, where I'm from."

"Are you as talented as he is?" she asked.

He shook his head. "Not by a long shot. Then again, I played cover songs to meet chicks. Ty writes his own lyrics and music, too. He's the real deal."

"Do you still play?"

"Not as often as I'd like. Running a company takes a lot of time and I like to see my family on occasion," he joked.

"You're married?"

"No, but Deena and I have been together for eight years. We've got two kids."

"Boys or girls?"

"One of each. Penny is five and Luke is three."

"You're lucky."

He gave her a sidelong glance. "How about you?"

"No," she said. "No family."

"Ty's a great guy," Paul said. "He seems to think you're pretty special."

Alexis felt her cheeks color. "Me? He said that?"

Paul wore a lazy grin. "He didn't have to."

"There's nothing going on," Alexis protested hotly. "I'm only here for the holidays."

"Pipe down, Lexi. I'm not accusing you of anything indecent. If two single people like each other, what's the harm?"

Alexis squirmed in her seat. She didn't mean to lose her cool.

He raised a thick eyebrow. "Maybe not so single?"

Alexis stiffened. She wasn't about to get personal with Paul, no matter how close he was with Tyler.

"It's not that simple," she said.

Paul sighed loudly. "Of course not. It never is. Deena was married when we met, so I'm not judging."

"It isn't like that," she objected.

He held up a hand. "Okay, I hear you. You're welcome to your secrets."

"Will I see you at any of Tyler's shows?" she asked, trying to steer the conversation back to neutral territory.

"Not unless you're staying into the new year." He pulled up to the marina and idled. He clearly wasn't opening any doors this time.

"I appreciate the ride, Paul. Thank you."

"No problem. I've done you a favor, now do one for me. Don't break my buddy's heart. He's one of the best people I know."

"I have no intention of breaking his heart."

"You know what they say about the best intentions."

"Merry Christmas, Paul," she said, grabbing her shopping bags and closing the door. Although Paul had touched a nerve, she liked the fact that Ty instilled such loyalty in his friends.

She dragged her bags to the water's edge and waited for the taxi. Glancing at her watch, she figured she'd have just enough time to make herself presentable before heading to The Galleon.

Chapter Seven

When Alexis left London for Mangrove Island, for once, she didn't have a grand plan. Life had reached the point where she had nowhere else to go except the place she'd spurned. Now that she was back, she was beginning to think it had been the right move. Even though her family fence mending had its obstacles, it no longer felt as insurmountable as it had back in London. Even her fight with Betsy didn't seem so horrible in hindsight. They yelled and said what they needed to say and somehow Alexis knew that her relationship with her sister would improve. And then there was Ty, such a welcome surprise. Alexis wished she could simply enjoy his company without the guilt that plagued her.

The minute she arrived at the house, she escaped to her room and dressed hurriedly in a black, sleeveless shift dress and black pumps. She ran a brush through her hair to tame the wild pieces. She told herself that she wasn't primping for Tyler; she was primping because she was going to a nice place like The Galleon and needed to look respectable. The Galleon was a beachside restaurant known for its unobstructed view of the incredible island sunsets. It had been many years since she'd enjoyed a sunset and she looked forward to it.

Tyler was already seated at an outside table when she arrived. Her cheeks burned as she felt his appreciative gaze travel from her bare legs up to her perfectly coiffed hair. When she reached the table, he stood up and pulled out her chair.

"Why thank you, kind sir," she said.

"I guess Paul got you back safely," he surmised.

"Paul's my hero."

"He's a great guy," he agreed. "I took the liberty of ordering your signature drink. I hope that's okay."

"Much needed, thank you."

"So things were that bad with your sister?" he prompted.

She waved him off. "It was a spat that needed to happen. Now, hopefully, we can make some progress."

"Good to know. Now we can enjoy the sunset before it's gone. Bet you don't get views like that in London," Tyler said, taking a moment to admire the disappearing view.

She turned her attention to the tangerine horizon streaked with red. Between the dreamlike sky and the sound of the waves lapping gently against the shore, Alexis felt her tension melt away.

"It's stunning," she said with a sigh.

"So are you," he said in a low voice.

Heat rose from her neck to her cheeks. "Ty…"

"I know, it's not a date." He leaned back in his chair, flashing that irresistible dimple in his cheek, and she couldn't deny the flutter in her stomach.

The waiter brought two whiskeys and set one in front of Alexis and the other in front of Tyler.

"You got one for yourself?" she queried.

"Why not? I could use a little more hair on my chest."

At the mention of his chest, Alexis's eyes inadvertently moved to admire his physique. When she caught herself staring, she immediately straightened in her chair and cleared her throat awkwardly.

"So have you had any other jobs aside from The Blue Heron and your music?" she asked. She hoped to distract herself from the hint of muscles lurking underneath his shirt.

"A couple, not too many."

"What's been the worst one?" she asked.

"Easy. Counting furniture in an insane asylum."

She threw her head back and laughed. "What? Is that even a job?"

"Paid eight dollars and fifty cents an hour, off the island naturally."

"Are you sure you weren't *in* the asylum?" she teased.

"I composed lyrics to one of my best songs in that place, so it was worth it. What about you?"

"I've never composed lyrics anywhere." She downed her whiskey and relished the burn as it spread through her body.

"Ha, ha. Your worst job, smart ass."

"Easy. Being a corporate lawyer."

"But that's what you do now."

"I've never had another job."

"Why would you do it for so long if you hate it?"

Alexis shrugged. "Lots of reasons."

"Is this the type of evidence you give at work?" he asked with a grin. "If so, I can see why the job might not suit you."

Alexis laughed despite herself. She didn't have the heart to tell him that corporate work did not involve giving evidence. "It offered me disposable income, respect, intellectual challenges. Lots of things I didn't have growing up."

"You know, most kids rebel by smoking dope or shoplifting. Not by becoming a lawyer."

"I wouldn't describe it as rebellion. The rebellion was cutting them off."

"What then?"

Alexis tried to decide how to explain her family to him. She couldn't even explain them to herself. They had always seemed so alien to her.

"I don't know. I just never felt like they were proud of me, like the things I did well weren't of interest to them."

"So what about Betsy? Why is she in the catbird seat?"

"She didn't reach above her station, for starters. Law is for superior people, or people who think they're superior."

"Doesn't your mother work for a lawyer?" he asked.

"The key phrase is works for. Truth be told, I think my

mom is fine with it. My dad's the one who equated lawyers with politicians and criminals."

Tyler nodded. "I know the type."

She sighed. "I bet your parents tell everyone who will listen what a talented musician you are. They probably have your songs on heavy rotation."

Tyler couldn't lie. His parents were great and he knew it. He tried to cover a guilty smile.

"So you've been practicing law for what, ten or eleven years? Why didn't you just get a new job when you realized you were miserable? Try a different kind of law?"

His line of questioning may have sounded critical coming from someone with less empathy, but from Tyler, it brought honesty and self-reflection bubbling to the surface.

"The truth is, I'd developed an identity, a persona that seemed to exist separate from the real me."

Tyler gave her a pitying look. "Well, I have to admit, I like you both. Real Alexis and Alternate Alexis. Like Coke Classic and New Coke."

"Oh, c'mon. Nobody liked New Coke."

"I have a confession," he said. "I liked Zima too."

She smiled. Now she knew he was lying, but she let him off the hook anyway. He reached under the table to squeeze her thigh and her body rippled with pleasure.

"Ty," she began and he immediately removed his hand. He recognized that tone of voice.

"Sorry, it just felt so natural," he said. His heart beat so loudly in his chest, he wanted to yell at it to be quiet.

She lowered her gaze, searching for the right words. "I am very attracted to you…" That was an understatement. "But I…I," she faltered.

He waved her off. "No buts. I like the first part of your statement. Let's stick with that." He gave her a devastating smile and her insides trembled.

"I really do like you, Ty, and trust me when I say I didn't think it was possible."

"Gee, thanks."

She realized what she'd said and her cheeks flamed. "Not that it was impossible to like you, specifically." She stumbled over her words. "That it was possible for me to like someone."

He grinned again and she realized that he was teasing her. "I could get used to this," he proclaimed. "A tongue-tied Alexis MacAdams."

"You have only yourself to blame."

"Good, I don't want you to blame anybody else but me. I want to be the one who ties your tongue."

She couldn't resist a smile. Staring at her across the table, admiring her lush hair as it blew gently in the breeze, Tyler Barnes felt like the luckiest guy in the world.

After feasting on lobster and scallops at The Galleon, Alexis and Tyler went to Lottie's Greenhouse to watch the skaters on the temporary ice rink. A Christmas tree loomed in the background, illuminating the festive atmosphere. Even though the weather rarely dipped below sixty degrees in winter, islanders loved invoking the look and feel of Christmas to the best of their abilities.

"It's pretty here, isn't it?" Tyler asked, entranced by their surroundings. "I mean, I'm sure London has its charms, but you can't ice skate with palm trees there."

"Anywhere but here. That was my motto."

"Why? I mean, I know opportunity knocked in London, but I'll bet it banged the hell out of your door and left a dent anywhere you went."

He meant to make her smile and was disappointed when she didn't. They'd had such a good time at dinner; he wanted to stoke those flames.

"London felt just far enough. I only needed one ocean."

He didn't press her for more. Patience was one of his virtues.

"I've always hated the nickname Ty," he said, seemingly out of the blue.

"What?" Alexis queried. She thought she'd misheard him.

"Kids from school used to call me Ty. I never shortened my name; people did it without asking. Even now, I cringe when anyone greets me as Ty. I know I'll never escape the name because it's part of my history, my past. And that's the thing about your past, it always catches up with you, no matter how much you want to bury it."

"But you introduced yourself to me as Ty."

"I assumed that's the name you would remember." He laughed. "That obviously didn't help."

"So you'd like me to call you Tyler?"

Tyler understood that she deliberately missed the point of his story. He caught her eye and held it, intense but not unnerving. "You can call me whatever you like. Anything sounds good rolling off your tongue."

Reddening slightly, Alexis turned her attention back to the skaters and laughed as a man fell over. "I'll stick with Tyler," she said finally.

"Do you want to take a spin?" he offered.

"No, thanks. I've only been skating once and it didn't go well."

"That's okay. I don't skate either, but I'm willing to make a fool of myself."

Alexis bit her lip, fighting a memory. The truth was that her one attempt at skating had been with Mark at one of the most amazing ice rinks in the world. Although the skating didn't go well, it was the night she'd realized that she was in love with Mark. She'd blocked Somerset House from her memory, but standing in Lottie's Greenhouse brought it all back to her in spades. She could almost feel Mark's arm around her waist.

Somerset House was the most grand and impressive ice rink imaginable. A twelve-feet tall Christmas tree and elegant neoclassical building adorned the backdrop. An English wonderland. Alexis remembered admiring the surroundings while watching skilled skaters dance their circles around the ice.

"This place is fantastic," she'd told Mark.

"One of London's many secrets. Now that I've revealed

one, it's your turn. Ladies' choice."

"For starters, I've never been ice skating so if that's why we're here…"

Mark had smacked his forehead comically. "But you came from the greater New York metropolitan area. Surely, you've been to Rockefeller Center."

"Only to laugh when people fall."

"Well, darling, it's time for the laugher to become the laughee."

"Those are not real words, you know. You're pretty inarticulate for a lawyer."

As usual, Mark had taken her barbs in stride. "No stalling, Miss MacAdams. We're going on that ice together. It's romantic, it's scenic, it's London at its best."

He glanced at her, realizing he hadn't won her over yet.

"You shall not fall," he assured her.

"Do we need to sign a waiver?"

Mark placed both hands on her shoulders and looked her squarely in the eye. "It will be my mission to ensure that one Alexis MacAdams does not fall on her perfectly shaped bum. An Englishman's honor."

He held up two fingers like a Scout.

"I think a bit of history will tell you everything you need to know about an Englishman's honor," Alexis quipped.

Mark's hands flew to his chest in mock injury and she laughed at his antics, never imagining what the future held for them.

She managed to make it once around the rink without

falling over. They were both too wrapped up in each other's company. Alexis recalled making a great effort to stay upright with Mark's hand supporting her waist. Just as she began to believe that all was well, she lost her balance and landed straight on her bottom. Mark immediately reached down and pulled her back up.

"Ten second rule," he said. "Doesn't count as a fall."

Alexis broke into a grin so wide that she could still feel it on her cheeks when she thought about it.

Alexis squeezed her eyes closed, unwilling to remember any more. Overwhelmed by a surge of emotion, she nearly keeled over. Thankfully, Tyler caught her by the elbow before she could topple and embarrass herself.

"One whiskey too many?" he joked.

"I'm sorry," she whispered. "I'm just tired. I haven't been sleeping well."

"Now it's my turn to be sorry," he remarked. "I practically kept you out at gunpoint."

"Don't be sorry," she told him. "I haven't been sleeping well for a long time. I have anxiety dreams." She felt silly saying it out loud. Before now, she'd only told her therapist who recommended sleeping pills. Alexis made no more appointments after that. She didn't want pills.

"Nightmares?"

"You could say that." She noticed that his hand was still gripping her elbow and she instinctively jerked away. Seeing Tyler's stricken face, she realized her mistake.

Alexis felt the knot in her stomach doubling in size. "I

didn't mean to do that," she said in a small voice. She offered her elbow. "Here, you can hold it again, if you want."

Tyler burst out laughing at the sheer absurdity. "Maybe I don't want to hold your elbow."

Alexis dropped her arm to her side. "Okay then."

"Maybe I'd rather hold some other body part."

She felt herself being drawn in by his intense gaze. "Which one?" she asked, daring him.

"Ladies' choice."

He gave her a cocky half-smile and she froze. Ladies' choice. Her thoughts flew back to Mark and the brief moment of pleasure immediately gave way to immense guilt.

"Tyler, I…" she faltered, uncertain what to say. "I'm scared."

"Scared?" He cupped her face with his hands. "Of me?"

"Of having feelings for someone other than my husband," she confessed.

His brow wrinkled in confusion. "Husband?" He edged back slightly. "Are you married?"

"Not anymore, but please Tyler, that's all I want to say about it for now." Tears filled her eyes, but Alexis was determined not to cry.

"What's his name?" asked Tyler. He didn't know why he asked that; it just slipped out.

"Mark."

"Did you meet him in London?"

"Tyler," she began, then relented. "Yes, I did. Now

please don't ask anything else. I've fashioned myself a nice, delusional bubble and I like it in here. It's cozy."

"Fine for you, but how do you expect anyone else to get in?" he asked.

She grew flustered. "I don't."

Without another word, she fled Lottie's Greenhouse. Away from Tyler and away from the good feelings he evoked. How could she flirt with him so shamelessly? How could she consider him as anything more than a friend? She continued to run through the quiet island streets as images of Somerset House raced through her mind. Every nervous giggle. Every smile.

The memory was too painful. She needed to keep moving because standing still made it too easy to think. She ran through Coconut Cove to the nearest beach, kicking off her shoes as soon as she hit the sand. She waded into the water, seeking absolution. The bottom of her dress quickly became drenched. The waves crashed against the cluster of boulders and Alexis welcomed the salt water spray on her face. She didn't deserve Tyler's attention. She didn't deserve to be happy. She'd had her chance at love and she blew it. She deserved to be exactly as she was – alone.

Chapter Eight

The next morning Alexis dragged herself to Owen's Nativity play along with the whole family. She'd been holed up in her bedroom ever since she returned from the beach the night before. Tilly could tell something was amiss and she tried in vain to piece together the mystery that was her daughter. Even though she was Alexis's mother, Alexis had always seemed slightly alien to her. She knew how to parent Betsy without thinking, despite the fact that Betsy was her first child; she found parenting Alexis far more challenging.

They took golf carts to St. Matthew's Church where Owen attended preschool. Alexis carefully chose a seat at the end of the row by the exit door. She made a habit of always sitting near an exit, whenever the option presented itself.

While they waited patiently for her nephew's shining moment, Betsy did a commendable job of keeping Joey occupied. Alexis realized how difficult basic errands must be for Betsy when Joey was involved. She didn't have attention for anyone or anything else, not that Alexis blamed her. No wonder Owen took such a liking to Alexis, though. She had unfettered time to sit and engage him in conversation and Owen was a kid who clearly liked conversation.

Despite Alexis's attempt to focus on the children on stage, her mind kept drifting to Tyler and her behavior at Lottie's Greenhouse. Gentleman that he was, he'd texted her last night to see if she was okay, but she couldn't bring herself to reply. How could she possibly explain herself without wrenching open the door to a conversation she absolutely did not want to have? She didn't need to relive her heartbreak and Tyler and her family didn't need to know any of it. Soon she'd be gone for parts unknown and they could all resume their lives before she so rudely interrupted them with her torment.

Finally, the Three Wise Men arrived to see the Baby Jesus. Alexis sighed inwardly with relief. Owen wore a white beard far too big and bushy for his small face. He also carried a walking stick much too tall for his four-year-old body. The pairing, however, made for an adorable effect.

"One of the Wise Men was a gimp?" she whispered to her mother.

"He thought his character needed a prop."

"Wouldn't that be frankincense or myrrh?"

The larger boy playing Wise Man One yelled, "We have followed a wandering star that has led us here."

"We bow before our King and offer our finest gifts to

the baby Jesus," said Wise Man Two, in a voice that was barely audible. He bowed down and basically pulled the other two Wise Men down with him.

"Peace to the world," declared Owen as Wise Man Three. "One day baby Jesus will be dead…but not while he's a baby."

The actors exchanged confused glances. This was clearly not in the script. Alexis watched as Betsy and Joe hid their eyes in embarrassment.

"Glory to God in the Highest," yelled Wise Man One in a brave effort to save the scene.

Mary raised the generic baby doll playing Jesus for the Wise Men to adore. The sight of the doll brought unexpected tears to Alexis's eyes. Quickly, she turned toward the wall so no one would notice. She pretended to move a stray hair from her face while wiping away an escaped tear. Her mother gave her a curious glance but turned her attention back to the stage.

When the play finished, the grown-ups jumped to their feet and clapped heartily. The children formed a line on stage and all bowed, mostly at the same time. Alexis noticed that the innkeeper seemed to have wet his pants. Owen bowed repeatedly until one of the teachers directed him off the stage.

Afterward, they all went to Betsy's house for lunch where the usual divide occurred. The men and boys wandered into the family room and the women ended up in the kitchen. Alexis had always hated that about her family; it was very hunter and gatherer. It was, in fact, the main reason she never wanted to learn to cook. She hated feeling like she'd been assigned to a room based on her gender and not because she showed an interest in being there.

Betsy took out rolls and cold cuts while Tilly set out the condiments. Alexis looked around for a job to do. She and Betsy hadn't addressed their mall fight and Alexis thought it best to keep quiet and make herself useful.

"Do you want me to get the plates?"

"Sure," Betsy said, without a trace of hostility. "Paper plates are in the pantry. There are red and green ones for Christmas."

Outside of Betsy's house, Alexis couldn't remember the last time she'd used a paper plate. Not since she left the island. It was such an odd thing to notice.

Tilly opened two beer bottles. "I'll bring these to the men," she said.

"Have you tried Tropic Turtle?" Alexis asked Betsy.

Betsy's eyes widened. "Have you?"

"The other night at Gatsby's. It was excellent."

"Gatsby's, huh? What brought you there?"

"I ran into an old friend and he invited me to watch him play his music there."

Betsy stopped in her tracks, a Kaiser roll in each hand. "Which old friend would that be?"

"Do you remember Tyler Barnes?"

At first Betsy stifled a chuckle, then decided to let it loose. The more clueless Alexis appeared, the harder Betsy laughed.

"It only took him what, seventeen years?"

Alexis bristled. She didn't like her sister laughing at her. It reminded her too much of their childhood.

"What are you talking about?"

"Tyler Barnes had a massive crush on you in high school. A monster-sized, nausea-inducing crush. How can you not remember that?"

"I don't think I can remember something I never knew."

"Then you were living more up your own ass than I ever realized. I'm surprised you didn't charge yourself rent."

Betsy carried on setting out the rolls, whistling Jingle Bells. Alexis remained still, trying to absorb what Betsy said.

"What makes you think he had a crush?"

"For starters, he used to ride his skateboard past our house all the time. Rumrunner Road wasn't on his way to anywhere. Hell, it's not on anyone's way to anywhere." She glanced over at her mother. "No offense, Mom."

Tilly shrugged. She was more interested in hearing the rest of the story.

"Okay, he rode his skateboard around the island. Big deal."

"He worked with you on the Yearbook Committee. How could you forget that?"

Alexis wrinkled her nose. "Lots of people worked on the Yearbook Committee. What does that prove?"

Betsy gave an exasperated sigh. "Tyler Barnes was not a

Yearbook Committee kind of guy. He was a lusted after hot guy with a guitar who didn't give other girls the time of day because of you."

"Then why did he never ask me out?"

"You'll need to ask him that, but I'd bet my money on pure intimidation. You're not exactly of the soft and cuddly variety."

Alexis shook her head, still in disbelief. "You remember all this? I can't even remember the name of my favorite teacher."

"It was Mrs. Baker, your English teacher. She said you had the eyes of Walt Whitman and the soul of Thoreau." Betsy scratched her head. "You ate that crap up."

Alexis stared at her sister, open-mouthed. "What the hell?"

Betsy shrugged like it was no big deal. "I still live here. Things like that get reinforced over the years just through casual conversation. I still cut Melissa Kinney's hair and she had a raging lust for Tyler even after high school, but he wasn't interested. She couldn't stand the sight of you in high school. Was happy as a clam that you left town, not that it helped her any."

"How sweet."

"I'm just giving you the background." Betsy gave her a pointed look. "You asked."

Alexis closed her eyes, absorbing the information. It all made sense, thinking about Tyler's eagerness to see more of her. His memory of her poetry. Then she thought of her behavior at the rink and the acidic taste of regret burned her throat.

"I'm a complete asshole," she whispered.

Betsy glanced up from her cold cut tray. "And that only took *you* seventeen years."

Alexis spent the remainder of her time at Betsy's obsessing over her sister's revelation. Finding out about Tyler's crush on top of her already deplorable behavior made Alexis feel worse than awful. Since she already felt awful on a regular basis, she had no desire to compound the negative feelings. When Owen asked her to take him to a nearby park, she jumped at the chance to get outside and clear her head.

"Would your brothers like to go?" she asked him.

Owen shook his head. "They think it's a baby park because it only has swings and monkey bars. Well, Brian says that anyway. Joey just doesn't like parks."

"Sounds like fun to me," said Alexis.

Once she cleared the excursion with Betsy, they walked the two blocks to the small park. Owen went immediately to a swing and plopped down in the seat.

"Would you like me to push you?" she asked.

"No. I like to sit here and watch for the birds."

Alexis gave him a knowing smile. "You don't actually play when you come here, do you?"

He shook his sun-kissed head. "No. It's quiet here. And I like bird watching. Some real colorful ones like to come to this park."

Alexis wanted to hug him in the worst way. He pulled a small bag from his pocket and held it up to Alexis.

"Want a cookie?"

"Where did you get those?" she asked.

"I always steal a bag from the pantry before I come to the park. They're chocolate chip." He tore open the bag and popped one in his mouth.

"I'll have one," she said, holding out her hand. He placed a small cookie in her palm and began to swing. "Thank you."

"You'll be here for Christmas, right?" he asked, his large, solemn eyes seeking reassurance. "It's only days away now!"

"Yes, definitely." She crunched away on the cookie. Even though it wasn't homemade, it tasted good. It tasted of her childhood.

"And then you'll disappear, like the dinosaurs."

"No, Owen. We're friends now, right?"

He nodded somberly.

"Then trust me when I tell you that won't happen again. My disappearing days are over."

Alexis noticed that the top of his bag had dipped toward the ground as he leaned forward and she reached down to tilt it back up.

"You've got to watch you don't spill your cookies everywhere." She laughed to herself. "I know that sounds like a euphemism for something naughty, but it isn't."

"What's a euphemism?"

"Um, like when you say one thing, but it really means something else."

"Like when Mommy says she's happy you're here."

Alexis gently squeezed his hand. "No, that's just a lie."

"Don't you like Nana and Grandpop?" he asked innocently. "Grandpop can be a little grumpy, but he's okay most of the time."

Alexis sighed. Owen had more insight than was necessary for a four-year-old.

"Nana and Grandpop are my parents and I love them," she insisted.

"I asked you if you *like* them," he said pointedly.

Alexis bristled. Now I see why I may have been somewhat of a thorn in my family's side, she mused.

"They're decent, hard-working people," she replied diplomatically.

"So you don't like them," he said. "That's okay. I don't always like them either, but I do love them."

He sang a little song to himself as he sat on the swing watching for birds, completely at peace with his feelings on the subject. Alexis wished she could simplify her feelings like that. She'd managed to create such layers of emotional complexity that she could scarcely function.

Alexis ruffled his hair affectionately. "I like you, that's for sure."

He grinned up at her and she noticed pieces of chocolate stuck to his small teeth. "You could be my best friend," he said. "I don't have one yet."

Alexis was touched. "I do have a vacancy in the best friend department."

"What about Tyler?" Owen asked.

Her eyes widened. "Where did you hear that name?"

"Mommy and Nana. And when Mommy mentioned him earlier, she said he was always coming to see you."

"He's definitely a friend," Alexis admitted, "but I'll reserve best friend status for you." She stole another cookie from his bag and he clutched the bag to his chest in mock outrage.

"Hey, no more sharing," he declared.

She lifted Owen out of the swing in a tickly hug. He giggled and wriggled until she was afraid he'd be sick.

"You should have kids," Owen told her. "Then I'd have someone fun like you to play with."

Alexis set him down and pressed her lips together.

"I'm generally not the kind of person other people describe as fun, Owen, but I'm glad you think so." She cleared her throat and forced a smile. "Now finish those cookies before I get you home so I don't get in trouble."

After returning Owen to Betsy's, Alexis made her escape. She couldn't stop thinking about Tyler and was determined to apologize for running off. She took a golf cart to The Blue Heron in the hope that he'd be working. Unfortunately, he wasn't behind the bar when she arrived.

"He's kayaking today," the younger guy told her. "Try Sandy Point."

"Thanks," said Alexis, uncertain whether to track him down. If he was enjoying a peaceful day of kayaking, who was she to ruin it with her presence?

"Are you Alexis?" the bartender asked.

Alexis's eyebrows shot up. "Yes."

The bartender grinned. "Okay, now I get it." He reached across the bar to shake her hand. "Lewis Moore."

"Nice to meet you, Lewis."

Alexis suspected that, unlike her, Tyler was in touch with his emotions and not afraid to share. There was, however, the somewhat salient point that he'd never expressed his feelings to the one person who seemingly mattered – Alexis. She may have been blind to his attention in school, but in her defense, he never actually told her how he felt. If he had, at the very least, she may have remembered him.

She hopped in her golf cart and sputtered off toward Sandy Point. She hadn't been to that part of the island since her arrival and she was curious to see how it looked after all these years. Lots of kids from school went kayaking and paddle boarding there, but Alexis had never been interested. She hadn't been interested in anything the local kids did. Because she had no desire to be a local kid, she did her best to distance herself from their activities.

When Alexis arrived at Sandy Point, she couldn't see a soul. She squinted into the distance as a lone figure appeared on the horizon. She watched his sure, fluid movements and knew in an instant that the figure was Tyler. She waved her arms and hopped up and down, hoping to draw his attention without looking ridiculous. As the kayak continued to move closer, Alexis felt confident that he'd seen her.

When he finally came close enough that she could see his face, Alexis felt tiny shockwaves throughout her body.

His dark blond hair was damp and wavy from the sea spray and his muscles rippled as he moved the paddle from side to side with decisive strokes. For a moment, she forgot why she was there.

He grinned when he saw her and she hurried toward the water's edge to meet him.

"Didn't expect to see you here," he called.

He effortlessly bounced out of the kayak and pulled it to the sand right near her feet. Alexis gaped as he unzipped the top of his wetsuit and slipped on a red wicking shirt that he pulled from his waterproof bag. Short of closing her eyes, she couldn't avoid noticing his muscular torso. Dry clothes did not do him justice.

"I just wanted to apologize for last night." She searched for the right words. "For running off like some kind of drama queen. It's so unlike me."

"No need to apologize," he said gently. "You're obviously working through some issues. I respect that."

Issues. Yes, she certainly had those. When she dared to meet his gaze, she realized that he was grinning from ear to ear.

"Why do you look so happy about my issues?"

He reached for her hand and gave it a squeeze. "Because last night you told me you have feelings for me."

Embarrassed by her inadvertent admission, she dug the tip of her shoe into the sand. "I didn't define those feelings. Maybe I meant friendly feelings. Or nostalgic feelings."

He continued grinning at her. "Don't think it can be

nostalgia considering your memory problems."

She couldn't help but smile back. "I am truly sorry I don't remember you from high school."

"Because you realize you missed out?" he asked, only half-joking.

"Maybe I missed out on a lot of things," she said truthfully. She didn't know whether it was Tyler's influence, the years away, or maybe a bit of both, but the island was starting to seem more appealing than it had to her younger self.

"Do you kayak or have you missed out on that, too?" he asked.

She shook her head. "Not really my thing."

"Would you like to try?"

She glanced at the kayak. "But it's only for one person, isn't it?"

His eyes narrowed seductively. "You can sit on my lap. Then you can feel all my moves."

Alexis groaned. "If you want me to erase you from my memory again, you're doing a good job."

"Do me a favor," Tyler said, unable to stop smiling.

"Not if it involves sitting on your lap."

"Get in the kayak," he commanded.

"Excuse me?"

"Not with me. Just you. I'll tell you what to do, but I'd like you to get out there and paddle around. Just see how it feels. I love to kayak when I need a release."

"Is that why you're kayaking today?" she asked. "You needed a release?"

He eyed her with a hunger she hadn't seen before. "Definitely."

"Alright then," she agreed. "I'll give it a try."

He held the kayak steady while she eased herself down into the seat. After a quick demonstration on how to use the paddle, he pushed her out to sea. Alexis moved the paddle from left to right, using strong strokes, and quickly picked up speed. As the kayak undulated through the ripple of waves, she was amazed how free she felt. The salt water sprayed her face and she found herself smiling at the expanse of sky in front of her. In fact, the clear sky ahead was all she could see. How could she have labeled kayaking as mundane? She cursed her arrogant teen self. Kayaking in the open sea was thrilling, almost as thrilling as the thought of Tyler's lips on her bare skin. Alexis shivered and chastised herself for letting such salacious thoughts sneak into her head. She had no right to fantasize about him. She took a deep breath and focused on paddling, following Tyler's instructions on how to turn the kayak so she could change direction. It took a bit of maneuvering, especially with the breeze, but she managed.

As she glanced to her right, she noticed a dorsal fin in the water and her stomach lurched. Another fin appeared. She quickly realized that there were at least six fins and they were curved rather than straight. A pod of dolphins. Her body relaxed and she stopped paddling to enjoy the view, wishing for a brief moment that she'd agreed to ride on Tyler's lap. It would have been nice to share this incredible moment with him. Suddenly one of the dolphins leaped out of the water and sailed through the air, splashing back into the water as it swam across the horizon. Alexis's smile widened as the other dolphins followed suit.

Once the impromptu show was over, she faced the beach and began to paddle in earnest. Tyler applauded her when she reached the shore.

"Those dolphins were trying to win you over," he said, pulling the kayak safely onto the sand.

"God, I could do that every day," she exclaimed, her eyes dancing with excitement. She didn't even bother to smooth her wild hair, despite the loose strands sticking to her cheeks.

"You sure could. You're a natural," he declared.

"It's amazing," she said, throwing her arms around him. Instantly she withdrew, her cheeks flushed. "I'm so sorry. I'm not trying to play games with you, Tyler, I swear. I want to explain everything at some point, but I'm just not ready."

"I'm a patient man, Alexis. I mean it," he said. He hesitated, debating whether to risk his next question. He didn't want to scare her off again. On the other hand, she had confessed to feelings, however vague they were.

"My friends are having a Christmas party tomorrow night. Friends from school actually, not that you'd remember them," he teased.

"Names?" she prompted.

"Craig was our year and his wife, Peyton, was the year after us. Craig Keeler."

She grimaced, ashamed not to remember Tyler's friend either. Peyton, however, she did remember.

"I played soccer with Peyton," she said.

Tyler high-fived her. "I hoped you'd get that one. She remembers you. Craig does, too. They'd love to see you." His blue eyes beckoned her and she felt her resistance fading.

Alexis sighed. "I feel so foolish, blocking out so many people. Like I wasn't paying attention to my life. I had no clue how self-obsessed I was."

"You were looking ahead instead of around you. Not living in the moment," he said. "A common mistake, but usually made by people on the mainland."

"Was I at least nice to you in school?" she asked, tipping up her chin to see him more clearly.

"You were always polite," he said. "You just kept to yourself. I used to try to sneak a peek at your notebook when we were in the library. I wanted to read some of your poems."

Alexis couldn't believe he'd wanted to read her poetry. She realized that she would've let him, if she had known. No one in her family had seemed interested. Just her English teachers.

"I'd be happy to share them now, if I knew where they were."

He slackened. "You didn't keep them?"

"I left here with a backpack the day after graduation," she told him. "No exaggeration."

"Well, if you ever decide to express your emotions

through the printed word again, I'm volunteering to read. As you know, I write lyrics so I'm always interested." He swept a hand gently over her hair and she shivered at his touch. "So will you come to the Keelers' party? I sure would like to ogle you in a pretty dress."

"I'll go," she relented. She wouldn't mind seeing Peyton again. She remembered the tall blonde as a talented soccer player with a fun-loving attitude.

"They live in Flamingo Key. White Oak Lane."

"Close to Gatsby's," she remarked. "No wonder you like playing there."

"Craig actually owns Gatsby's."

Alexis's eyebrows shot up. "You're kidding."

"People manage to eek out a living here, despite your misconceptions," he teased.

Her face grew hot. "I never thought this place was a dead end," she objected. "I just didn't think it suited me."

"And?"

"And what?"

"Do you still think it doesn't suit you?"

She found the strength to hold his gaze and quickly began to lose herself in the depths of those blue eyes. "I don't know anymore, Tyler. I feel like I'm seeing this place for the first time. Maybe what didn't suit me then, might suit me now."

Chapter Nine

"So if we're going to bake the Good Housekeeping cake, we'd better do it soon," Tilly said as she and Alexis folded laundry at the kitchen table.

"I thought you decided it was Betsy's thing," she replied. Alexis didn't want to piss off her sister anymore than she already had.

"It's fine," her mother assured her. "Betsy has enough on her plate. She'll be thrilled to have a year off."

Alexis focused on the pair of socks in her hand. "Don't let me ruin any of your traditions. I know I haven't been around much, or at all."

"Oh Alexis, you're being ridiculous. It's good to do things you're not good at. Keeps you humble." Tilly grabbed the laundry basket with the folded items and huffed her way out of the room.

Alexis fumed inwardly. Lack of ability had nothing to do with it, not that her mother would believe that. Alexis stared at her mother's outdated kitchen, the same butter yellow kitchen that Alexis remembered from childhood, and had a sudden urge to see her own kitchen in London. Well, it wasn't hers anymore because she'd sold the flat, but still. She didn't think it was possible to miss a kitchen, but she missed hers. She pictured it in her mind, the whiteness of it. The appliances were state-of-the-art, a real chef's kitchen. Initially, she hadn't been sure her skills warranted such a kitchen, but Mark had insisted. He liked to cook as well and had convinced her that they wanted the best, if only for resale value.

Alexis remembered the wholesome smell of fresh banana muffins as they baked in her sleek, stainless steel oven. She pictured her burgeoning belly, how she'd looked forward to the day when she'd have a child who banged on pots and begged to lick the wooden spoon.

"Baking again, huh?" Mark had asked, appearing in his pajamas. "Must be the nesting instinct."

He'd sidled up behind her and wrapped his arms around her newly expanding belly. She had gotten to the point where her regular clothes no longer fit comfortably.

"I find baking more calming than cooking. There's too much multi-tasking when you're cooking."

"I shall have to remember to thank my wonderful mum for taking you under her culinary wing. To think when I met you, you couldn't boil an egg." He'd kissed her neck and delved into the refrigerator for juice.

"I would love to pretend you're exaggerating. And if you say that in front of anyone, I will pretend."

"Come on, love. You wore your lack of domesticity like a badge of honor. I hardly think you'd be embarrassed."

That was true. She had.

"I wouldn't want anyone to think I didn't cook because I can't. I'd rather they think it's because I won't."

"Point taken." He kissed her lightly on the nose. "Let's enjoy these weekends whilst we can because once this little bundle of joy muscles her way in, it'll be a sleepless and muffinless world we live in."

"I've been thinking about something."

"Uh oh."

"Now hear me out. What would you think if I decided to leave my job after the baby is born?"

She knew that those were not words Mark had ever expected to come out of his wife's mouth.

"Seriously?"

Alexis rubbed her belly almost defensively rather than affectionately. "Yes. I've been feeling panicky and unsettled lately and I think it's because I'm worried about leaving the baby."

"What about blasting off the glass ceiling?"

"I know, I know. I'm baking muffins and contemplating leaving the work force. Worst feminist ever."

Mark kissed her sweetly. "Are you worried the nanny will give her chocolate too soon? Or that she'll text her boyfriend all day whilst the baby swings from the drapes?"

"I worry about all of it. That no one will look after it as well as me."

He lifted her chin slightly and looked into her hazel eyes. "It's totally your decision. I'm happy either way."

"Thank you. That means a lot."

"Besides, if the baby's anything like you, you'll be running back to work in no time."

Alexis swatted his arm. "You'd better watch it, pal. If this kid's anything like me, you're going to want me on your side when it's old enough to argue."

"So that buys me, what, another year before I need to make nice?"

"You just lost your banana muffins to Hal."

Alexis swallowed hard, staring at her mother's yellow, electric oven. She would never bake another muffin in her beautiful white kitchen. More importantly, she would never bake another muffin for Mark. Why had she not left her job that very day? Maybe it would have saved a lot of heartache. Why had she put her career above everything else? It was all she could do not to burst into tears.

Tilly placed the laundry basket at the bottom of the stairs and came back into the kitchen, oblivious to her daughter's torment.

"Why don't we do it now?" Alexis proposed. She wanted, needed to move forward. To make new memories. She didn't want to live the rest of her life feeling haunted by a life that no longer existed.

Tilly pulled a large mixing bowl from the cupboard. "Okay then. If you're sure."

"I don't have to be at the party until eight."

"A party?" Tilly repeated, grabbing bags of flour and sugar from the pantry.

"Yes, a Christmas party at the Keelers. He owns Gatsby's."

"Keeler? Somebody you went to school with?"

Alexis nodded as she retrieved the wooden spoon from the cutlery drawer. "I played soccer with his wife, Peyton."

"I never could keep up with all those names," Tilly admitted. "There were dozens of girls on your soccer team."

"It's not like you came to any games," Alexis pointed out.

"Only because you didn't want us to," Tilly protested. "Dad couldn't have because of his work schedule, but I could have arranged it with Morris."

Alexis didn't remember telling her mother not to come to games, but it certainly sounded like the kind of thing she'd have said. In her defense, she was a teenager. She didn't even like soccer all that much, but it was an excuse to be out of the house. Most of her after-school activities were motivated by a desire to avoid being at home. She'd never felt like she could be herself there; someone was always on hand to criticize her books or make her feel different from the rest of the family. Home for Alexis had never been the haven that it was meant to be.

Tilly turned up the Christmas classics while she read through the cake recipe.

"What would you like me to do?" asked Alexis.

"Let me see what's easy," she replied, scanning the recipe.

Alexis sighed. Deliberate or not, she was tired of the

condescension. "I can do any of it, Mom. It won't be the first cake I've made."

Tilly raised an eyebrow. This was news to her. "Terrific. You can do the whisking for me."

She handed a mixing bowl and a whisk to Alexis before moving to the cupboard for ingredients.

"So how did you learn to bake?" Tilly asked.

"Someone taught me."

"Someone? You mean like those chefs that come to your house? I saw that on TV once. One of The Real Housewives, I think. I didn't recognize the names of half the ingredients she used. I mean, what's the big deal with gluten?"

"Moira, my mother-in-law," Alexis interjected. "That's who taught me."

Tilly stopped, her hand hovering mid-air, clutching a box of flour. Alexis knew this news would rattle her mother, but she felt the need to tell her anyway. Tilly placed the flour on the counter, her eyes burning a whole into the cardboard. She was afraid that if she looked at her daughter's face, she'd crumble.

"And when exactly did you acquire a mother-in-law?" Tilly asked calmly.

"Six and a half years ago."

"If you're married, why aren't you wearing a ring?" Tilly glanced at her naked finger. "And more to the point, where's your husband?"

Alexis felt her entire body tense up. "It's not something I'm ready to discuss."

Try as she might, Tilly couldn't bear the betrayal. It was bad enough that Alexis had shut them out over the years, but to marry someone and not even have the decency to inform her own parents? What else was she hiding?

Tilly shifted the box of flour away from the edge of the counter and retreated from the room without another word. Alexis stood with the whisk still in her hand, uncertain whether to follow. Although she wasn't ready to discuss Mark, she no longer wanted to bury all of her emotions. She needed to start some type of dialogue with her mother, however uncomfortable.

Alexis found her mother in her parents' bedroom. Tilly sat alone on the bed holding a piece of embroidery. Alexis was struck by the appearance of the room. It hadn't changed a bit in seventeen years. Same floral bedding, same beige blinds with matching floral curtains, same magnolia white paint. The room was neat and tidy with a place for everything and everything in its place. She seemed to have inherited something from her mother, even if it was a simple de-cluttering gene.

Alexis knocked on the half-open door. "Mom, can I talk to you?"

"I sure wish you would," her mother replied. "Your silence has been deafening."

"I'm sorry that I've hurt you. Truly."

Tilly placed her embroidery to one side and removed her reading glasses before turning her attention to her daughter. "Tell me, Alexis. Did we abuse you?"

Alexis could already see where this was going. "No."

"Did we neglect you?"

"Not legally."

Tilly stiffened. "I don't really know what that means."

Alexis sat down beside her on the bed. She wanted to explain herself in a way that wasn't hurtful to her mother, but she didn't know how.

"It means you gave me food, shelter, and all the necessities I needed."

"That sounds like a good start," said Tilly. "It's more than a lot of kids get. Don't you see those commercials with the poor, starving children? They look like they're on death's door."

Alexis steadied her breathing, not wanting to lose patience with her mother. This conversation was too important and too long in coming.

"So do you think you played your parental parts and I'm some ungrateful spawn who spurned you and left you in the dust?" Alexis asked.

"I wouldn't put it quite like that." Tilly folded her arms across her chest. "I'd like to know what we didn't give you that you feel so strongly you should've had."

"Encouragement. Acknowledgment. A real sense of family."

Tilly bristled. "We encouraged you to do well."

"But not too well. That's just showing off, right? It was like you were all embarrassed to have a brainy kid in the family, but at the same time, you acted like I wasn't capable of being anything else. So basically you put me in

121

a box and then punished me for being there. And God forbid I had the nerve to stray from my box."

"What's all this talk about boxes?" her mother asked with a furrowed brow.

"I feel sorry for Owen already," Alexis said. "He's only four and you're doing the same thing to him. Imagine what he'll feel when he's fourteen."

"Or thirty-five?" Tilly asked.

"You made me feel like I didn't belong, not here and certainly not as part of this family," she admitted hotly. "What can I say? You wore me down."

"So the MacAdams are a box-wielding bunch of degenerates who reject any family members displaying signs of brain activity. Is that your opinion?"

As Alexis expected, her mother did not grasp her daughter's point of view.

"Not exactly…"

"Well, you're a big shot corporate lawyer now," Tilly shot back, her face and neck flushed with anger. "What do you care what the little folks think?"

"Stop with the big shot lawyer crap, Mom," she spat. "I actually hate my job."

Tilly blinked. "You do?"

"See? You're surprised. You think a cold, heartless job suits me perfectly." Alexis leapt off the bed in frustration. "You don't even know me." She trailed off, fighting back tears.

"So it's our fault that you hate your job?" Tilly snapped. "I guess it's our fault that you no longer seem to have a husband. Is this some kind of early mid-life crisis?"

Alexis grimaced. "I'm trying my best to explain myself to you, Mom. To share how I feel. Do you have any idea how hard this is for me?"

"Sounds like blame to me." Tilly's thin lips clamped together like a petulant child's. She didn't want to hear anymore. She was thankful her husband wasn't around for this nonsense. Greg would've hit the roof.

Alexis shook her head sadly. "I don't think you want to know. You would rather assume, the way you have always assumed things about me. You never wanted to know the real me. Why bother when you already have your own version of me, right?"

Refusing to cry in front of her mother, Alexis couldn't escape the room fast enough. Tilly stared blankly at the empty doorway, wondering where she went wrong.

When Tilly walked into the kitchen two hours later, her eyes red with emotion and fatigue, she stopped short. On the countertop rested the completed Good Housekeeping cake. It was perfect.

Chapter Ten

Betsy had just finished up with Heather, the local dental hygienist and her last customer of the day, when Alexis entered the salon. The surprise on Betsy's face didn't go unnoticed.

Alexis sat down in the small waiting area and admired the tasteful interior. Not trashy with loud music. More of an oasis.

Heather paid in cash, which Betsy appreciated. "Thanks, Heather. Enjoy the party. You look like a million bucks."

"That's why I only come here," Heather said with a girly wink.

Once Heather departed, Betsy sauntered over to the waiting area, slightly tense.

"Hi. Nice place," said Alexis.

"Thanks. Holiday party season is a big boost. Why are you here? Lip wax?"

"My sister runs a successful salon. I thought I should check it out in person." Alexis surveyed the creamy walls and small water feature. Different from the country style that dominated Betsy's home, more serene.

"So?" Betsy prompted.

"It's not what I expected," Alexis admitted.

"Well, I'm not an apple either, you know." Betsy placed an indignant hand on her ample hip.

"You are more pear-shaped," Alexis said, unable to resist tormenting her sister.

Betsy narrowed her eyes and Alexis responded with a wicked smile. It was a smile Betsy remembered all too well and one she'd missed more than she cared to admit.

"So what's it like running your own business?" asked Alexis.

Dropping her guard, Betsy plopped down on the arm of the chair. "Hard work. And the kids are hard work. And my marriage is hard work. But it's all worth it."

"Good for you," Alexis said genuinely.

"Mom seemed a little upset when I talked to her earlier. Did you two have an argument or something?"

"Or something." Alexis sighed. "I told her a bunch of things she didn't want to hear. There may have been raised voices involved."

"Seems to be going around."

"I needed to get some things off my chest, just like you did," Alexis said, finally acknowledging their mall fight.

"Well, I felt better after I got that out of my system," Betsy said with a smirk. "How about you?"

"It's different with Mom. She just doesn't see my point of view and I honestly think she's not being stubborn. I think she genuinely has a different version of events."

"Like she has a different version of you?"

Alexis glared at her sister. "Shit Betsy, does she come to you with everything?"

"Who else does she have?"

"Well, the infamous Good Housekeeping cake is done, in any event. So you're off the hook." She glanced at Betsy and noticed tears glistening in her brown eyes. "What's wrong? Did you actually want to bake the cake?"

Betsy wiped away a stray tear. "Not particularly. Baking with Mom is a pain, to be honest. We have different styles, as you may have noticed. But I do miss baking in general. The salon takes up so much of my time and then I'm exhausted by the time I get home and make dinner, clean up, the whole nine yards." She groaned in frustration.

"How did you end up with a salon anyway? You used to talk about opening a bakery on the island. Sugar-n-Spice needs a little competition. The island is just too big for one bakery."

Betsy covered her face with her hands. "I don't know! I don't know!" She threw her arms out in exasperation. "I got sucked in. But I'm making decent money now and we need it for Joey. He's going to need full-time care when he's older. I'd be crazy to walk away and start over."

"I guess Joe's not much of a helper."

"Look, I know he's a lot like Dad," said Betsy. "I'm not an idiot. Thankfully, we have Mom and Dad and Joe's parents around to help out. I couldn't do it all without help and I'm not ashamed of that."

Alexis gave her sister a light kick in the shin. "You think I would want you to be ashamed? Get over yourself. I get tired just thinking about your day because it doesn't end when you go home."

"Sandy Ventura was interested in partnering with me on the salon at one point, but I turned her down."

"Why?"

Betsy shrugged. "Didn't want to give away any control."

Alexis chuckled. "I guess we both got that trait from Mom." Her brow creased. "Why don't you consider it now? Let Sandy buy a percentage of the salon so that you can start another venture. Let Sandy run the day-to-day here."

Betsy eased out of the chair. "Sounds too complicated, not to mention expensive."

"No, it's really not," Alexis objected, her lawyer brain kicking in. "Let me draft some scenarios for you and then decide whether you want to move ahead."

"Draft your little heart out," Betsy agreed. "I'll take a look."

"Would you do me a favor in return?" Alexis asked sheepishly.

"Bartering, are we?" She crossed her arms. "What is it?"

"Would you do my hair in one of those pretty updos?" She pointed to a poster of a hair model on the wall.

"Now?"

"I'm going to a party and I'd like to look less corporate,

more Christmas."

"Sounds like a good party. Sure, I'd do it even if we weren't bartering." She walked over to one of the chairs and patted the seat. "Hop in."

"Are you sure you don't mind? I know you were ready to leave."

"If my little sister is making public appearances on the island, I want to at least hear that she looked spectacular."

Alexis slid into the seat and Betsy began to brush her hair. "Joe and I are actually going out on Thursday night for the union Christmas party. Mom and Dad were going to watch the kids, but Owen asked whether you would do the honors."

Alexis was surprised but pleased. "Really?"

"If you're around. I don't know what your plans are."

"No plans. I would love to."

Betsy pulled and twisted Alexis's hair, sticking clips in as she moved from one section to another. "I call him Alex sometimes, you know."

"Who?"

"Owen. He reminds me a lot of you when you were little."

"No wonder I've taken such a shine to him," Alexis said, glad that her sister was aware of their similarities. She hoped Betsy would do better than her own parents.

"Maybe you can talk him out of this obsession with death. The pediatrician says it's normal, but I still think he's a bit young for it."

Alexis stiffened. "I don't think I'd be the right person

for that."

In the mirror, Betsy looked at her quizzically but didn't pursue it. "Well, he's a bright little button, no doubt about it."

An idea occurred to Alexis. "I may invite a friend to hang out with me, if you don't mind."

"Sure, my house is always chaos. What's another body?" She arched an eyebrow. "And do you really need to say a friend? I mean, it's Tyler, right?"

Alexis blushed.

"So what's the deal with you two? People have spotted you all over the island together. You're a hot topic."

"Slow news week?" One thing Alexis didn't miss about her hometown was the rumor mill. Somebody always in your business. She figured that was a big reason she kept private matters to herself; she hated the scrutiny.

"Nobody said anything bad," Betsy clarified. "They mostly seem thrilled to see Tyler happy with someone. He's such a catch."

Alexis shook her head. "He's not with me. We're just friends."

"Sure thing," said Betsy in a way that suggested otherwise. "It's nice karma for him, though. Watching him pine over you in school was awful." She clucked her tongue in dismay. "Let's just say I'm glad Joe and I were very open with our feelings for each other."

"Yep, I remember you being very open in the front seat of his golf cart."

"We were hot for each other," she said simply.

"Nothing wrong with that."

For the first time in thirty-five years, Alexis envied the beautiful simplicity of her sister's life. She had a loving husband, three children, her own business and she managed it all. Alexis wondered why she'd overlooked her sister's good qualities for so long.

"Ta da," Betsy said, giving her sister's head a quick spray to keep the stray hairs in place. "What do you think?"

Alexis examined the result in the oversized mirror. Her long, brown hair was swept up in a lush, chocolate swirl that made Alexis feel both sexy and elegant. "It's perfect."

"Tyler will die," Betsy said, without noticing the wince that followed.

"Thank you," Alexis said softly. "I'll see you on Thursday, if not before."

Chilled by the winter breeze, Tilly wandered down the hall into Alexis's bedroom to retrieve a blanket from the bottom drawer of the dresser. She knocked out of habit, even though she knew that Alexis wasn't there. When she opened the drawer and moved the blanket, unfamiliar items caught her eye. A velvet box and a flash of red. Tilly eyed the box more closely. Her maternal instinct kicked in and she opened it. A beautiful wedding band sparkled inside. Had she left him? Tilly wondered. Maybe he cheated. She watched a few reality programs and she knew how slimy those husbands of successful wives could be. All those hours Alexis worked at the firm, any man would feel like a second-class citizen.

Her attention moved to the red item underneath. Curious, she unfolded it on the floor and gasped, her hand flying to cover her mouth. An infant Santa suit. Tilly smoothed out the wrinkles of the suit.

"Oh, Alexis," she said sadly.

In that moment, all of Tilly's anger and resentment toward her younger daughter dissipated. She'd been so busy justifying her own hostile feelings that she hadn't been willing to consider her daughter's, not even after her earlier tirade. Tilly was ashamed of her behavior. She should've known how difficult it was for Alexis to return home after all these years, not to mention how desperate she must have felt. No one could argue they had a close relationship so for Alexis to take time from her important job to travel across an ocean…Tilly shook her head woefully and carefully placed the items back where she found them. She remained on the floor of the bedroom, clutching the blanket and feeling like the worst kind of failure. Her daughter had seen fit to exclude her own mother from her life, to experience major life events without her family. Maybe it was high time that Tilly took a good, hard look in the mirror. She'd never considered herself a bad mother before, but she was beginning to see herself from Alexis's point of view and, she had to admit, it wasn't a pretty picture.

Chapter Eleven

Alexis dressed for the party, hoping to make a good impression but with seemingly little effort. She chose a dark green dress with a flattering draped cowl neckline that she'd bought from Liberty, her favorite store in London. It fell to just above the knee, short enough to show off her legs, yet long enough to maintain a modest appearance. The bodice hugged her curves. Sexy and graceful. She wore diamond stud earrings and painted her lips a deep red. It was actually pleasant to dress up for a change, to spend time on her appearance. The last time she dressed up was for a work function and, quite frankly, she didn't make as much of an effort. Alexis guessed that Tyler would be more appreciative of her labors than a room full of corporate hacks.

She fervently hoped the party would lift her spirits. The argument with her mother was still rattling around in her brain, not to mention the added stress of seeing people from high school. She anticipated the questions that would likely arise. Questions like 'what in the hell have you been doing for the past seventeen years?' 'Why have you never visited before now?' 'Doesn't your family miss you?' Caught up in her own emotional turmoil, she hadn't considered how normal conversation might put her on the spot.

On her way out, she debated whether to bypass the kitchen. She hadn't seen or spoken to her mother since their blowout and she wasn't sure if her mother was still upset. In the end, she decided to put on her big girl pants and say goodbye. As she stepped into the kitchen, her mother gave her an appraising look from behind the refrigerator door.

"That's a special dress," Tilly said, unable to keep the admiration out of her voice.

"It's for a festive occasion."

"I should hope so." Tilly closed the fridge door. "Would you like a snack before you go?"

"I'm sure they'll have food."

"Yes, but you'll probably be too busy talking to eat," Tilly commented.

"I'll eat, I promise."

"You did a wonderful job on the cake," her mother said. "I'm sorry I didn't get to help you."

"Thanks, but I didn't need help." Alexis reddened, wishing she could snatch back that last remark. She knew her mother hadn't mentioned help as a way of undermining her. It would be a long road before they could reach an accord, she realized.

"Did Betsy do your hair?" Tilly asked.

"She did. It's nice, don't you think?"

"Beautiful. I have two talented and beautiful daughters." She pretended to examine her nails. "I'm sorry you feel that we let you down. That wasn't our intention."

"I didn't come here to live in the past," Alexis said truthfully. "I'm willing to work on our relationship if you are."

"You're my daughter. Of course, I am."

Softening, Alexis gave her mother an impromptu kiss on the cheek which neither expected. "Don't wait up."

"Have a nice time, dear."

Alexis popped her head into the family room to say goodbye to her father, but he was snoring away in his chair. She placed her wrap around her shoulders and headed out the door.

Alexis had rejected Tyler's offer to pick her up so she could arrive a bit later. In part, she wanted to give him time alone with his friends, but, more than that, she felt that arriving together implied they were a couple.

She drove her mother's golf cart to the Flamingo Key neighborhood on the south side of the island. The house was closer than Gatsby's and she found it easily. Navigating Mangrove Island wasn't difficult at the worst of times. It was a far cry from the higgledy piggledy streets of London. Sometimes she wondered how she managed to find anywhere in that sprawling metropolis. Initially, she'd found it exciting to explore the forgotten side streets and cobblestone alleyways. Over time, it became a nuisance to live in a city without a grid system where, even after years of living there, she continued to carry a city map with her at all times. She appreciated Mangrove Island's simplicity now in a way that she hadn't before.

The Keeler house was obvious as soon as she turned the corner onto White Oak Lane. It was the house with about twenty golf carts parked in front of it, some on the neatly manicured lawn. Alexis hoped that Tyler wasn't one of the thoughtless guests to damage those lovely blades of grass. Somehow, she knew that he wasn't. She heard noise from the backyard but couldn't see over the tall fence.

On the way to the front door, she stopped to smooth her dress and unpeel a few stray hairs from her cheek. Then she took a deep breath and forged ahead.

The party was crowded, spilling out into the backyard where lights blazed and various outdoor games were set up. No one seemed to recognize Alexis so she maneuvered her way through the house with a smile plastered on her face but no actual conversation. She spied Tyler immediately, a beer in one hand and a horseshoe in the other. He was mid-throw when he saw her through the sliding glass door and he nearly clocked the guy next to him with the end of the horseshoe.

Seeing Tyler's reaction, Alexis allowed herself the tiny thrill of knowing that she was still desirable. She'd spent the last year and a half feeling more like a ghost than a person and Tyler's rapt attention somehow made her feel corporeal again.

She heard the grumbles of dismay when Tyler

abandoned his game to join Alexis in the house.

"I'm so glad you came," Tyler said, giving her a peck on the cheek. He desperately wanted to slide a hand around her waist, but he kept himself in check.

"Me too," she said with a genuine smile.

That smile took his breath away. He spotted Peyton in the kitchen, setting out a tray of brownies, and waved. Peyton set down the tray and worked her way through the throng of guests to greet Alexis.

Alexis recognized her instantly. Peyton looked surprisingly similar to her high school self, her tall frame still willowy and her blonde hair flowing around her shoulders in soft waves. She wore a red maxi dress with a halter style neckline that highlighted her toned shoulders and arms.

"Alexis, how great to see you again." Peyton greeted her with a warm hug and Alexis felt her stomach unclench. She hadn't realized just how anxious she was.

"You too, Peyton. You look absolutely beautiful."

"Forget me. You look stunning. Green is definitely your color."

"I love your house," Alexis said, glancing around the rooms again. "I wouldn't have expected such a modern interior from the outside."

"I know. I love that element of surprise. The house was a total mess when we bought it, so I couldn't wait to change it up."

"You did an incredible job."

Alexis felt something brush past her leg and looked

down in time to see a blonde blur disappear behind Peyton's dress.

"Ariana, you're supposed to be in bed, young lady," Peyton said firmly.

Alexis saw the little girl's fingers clasp her mother's legs.

"It's too dark," Ariana complained. She peeked out from behind Peyton and gazed up at Alexis with wide, light eyes. Her hair was lighter than Peyton's but with the same thick waves.

"Hello, I'm Alexis," she said. "And you are most definitely your mother's daughter." She bent down to speak to the little girl at her own level. "I'm guessing you're about five years old."

Ariana nodded mutely.

"Good guess," Tyler murmured.

She'd forgotten he was even standing there; she was so transfixed by the little girl. "Your nightgown is so lovely."

The little girl wore a long-sleeved, white nightgown adorned with pink and purple butterflies.

"I got it for my birthday," Ariana said.

"And when was that?" Alexis asked.

"October fifth."

A strong pair of arms swooped in and lifted Ariana off the ground. She screeched with delight as she was turned upside down.

"Craig, don't get her hyper now," Peyton warned. "It's bedtime."

Alexis straightened up and took a good look at Craig Keeler. Nope, he didn't seem familiar either. That made her feel a little better about not recognizing Tyler.

"Hi, Alexis," said Craig. "Long time, no see."

"Thank you for including me tonight," she said.

"Are you kidding? Tyler would've dropped me on my head in the middle of Mangrove Pass."

Tyler cleared his throat awkwardly. "Um, right here, Keeler." He ran a nervous hand through his hair.

Craig patted his daughter's back affectionately. "Let's get this specimen back to the lab, Doctor."

Ariana squealed as he flipped her the right way up. "Again, Daddy," she cried.

"To bed," Peyton said firmly.

"Goodnight, Ariana," said Alexis. "It was really nice to meet you."

"Goodnight, pretty lady," said Ariana. "Uncle Tyler talks about you all the time now. It's so boring." She rolled her large eyes for effect.

As Alexis suppressed a coy smile, Tyler felt that familiar ache. Her body in that curve-hugging dress was wreaking havoc on his usual restraint. The hint of her breasts, the nape of her neck, those long legs. Every inch of her turned him on. He was going to struggle to stay sane in her presence tonight.

"Sorry about that, Tyler," Peyton apologized for her daughter.

"No worries. It's not like I hide it very well." Tyler took a swig of beer.

"Well, when he mentioned he'd run into you," said Peyton, "I'll admit I was curious to see if he'd finally pluck up the courage to ask you out."

"I bet him twenty bucks that he'd crash and burn," Craig said, reappearing behind his wife.

"Spoken like a true friend," Tyler said.

"Oh, Alexis, forgive my manners," Peyton said. "Can I get you a drink or something to eat? Wine or beer?"

"I wouldn't mind a glass of wine. Red, if you have it."

"Is Pinot Noir okay?"

"Perfect."

As Peyton moved back into the kitchen for the wine, Craig stepped forward to continue to mortify his friend.

"So has Tyler played you any of his songs?" asked Craig, a glimmer of mischief in his eyes.

"I heard him play at your place, actually," said Alexis. "Congratulations on that, by the way, Gatsby's is a great place."

"Thanks, Peyton and I work our butts off, but we love it." He gave Tyler a sidelong glance. "Did he play Mermaid's Kiss?"

Tyler shot his friend a warning look that Alexis pretended not to see.

"Um, I don't think so. The title doesn't ring a bell."

"Oh, maybe next time. You should request it. Or Goodbye Girl. Now that's a classic."

"Pinot noir for our special guest," Peyton said, handing a long-stemmed glass to Alexis.

"Just in time," Tyler said through clenched teeth. As his best friend, Craig seemed to enjoy Tyler's discomfort a bit too much.

"Thank you," Alexis said, careful not to spill the wine on her dress.

"Should we go outside?" Peyton suggested. "The air is perfect tonight."

"Sorry about that," he whispered, as they trailed behind the Keelers.

Tyler squeezed her hand and an electric current shot through her body.

"He's just having a good time making you squirm. I think it's pretty funny, actually."

Tyler sighed inwardly. He knew Craig was dying to bust his balls, but he didn't want his dream girl frightened off in the process. He was lucky enough to have this second chance at winning her and he wasn't about to have that chance scuppered by a well-meaning, albeit annoying, friend.

"So what have I missed out in Tyler's life?" asked Alexis good-naturedly, once they were seated on the patio. "I want all the embarrassing details."

Craig eagerly rubbed his hands together.

"Play nice, Craig," his wife warned him. She turned back to Alexis. "As everyone here knows, Tyler is obsessed with his music and with good reason."

"Yes, he's very talented," Alexis agreed. "I was afraid he'd be awful and I'd have to find a way to sneak out and never see him again."

Tyler looked at her with mock indignation and she gave him a sly smile in return, taking a delicate sip of her wine. She'd been a wine drinker for a long time, until whiskey had taken over. She'd forgotten how pleasant it felt to have a nice, smooth drink and be sociable.

Their exchange didn't escape Peyton's attention. To her, they seemed to act very much like a couple, whether they realized it or not.

"He spends time outdoors whenever the mood strikes him," Craig offered. "That's why he's a better surfer than me, that bastard."

"I don't have a wife to cater to, a child to chase after, or a business to run," Tyler said diplomatically.

"You could've had any of those things," Craig countered. "Not like you didn't have the chance."

They fell silent and Alexis sensed a sore subject had inadvertently cropped up.

"Is she coming tonight?" Tyler asked.

Craig shook his head. "She's visiting our grandma in Orlando for Christmas. Grandma Mabel's too old to travel now." Craig turned to Alexis, not wanting to exclude her. "My little sister, Shelby, had a thing for Tyler. Took her a long time to realize that he wasn't going to change his mind about her."

"It wasn't a reflection on her," Tyler added.

Craig patted his friend on the back. "I was pissed off, as Tyler well knows, but I got through it and so did she, eventually. I know there's somebody out there for her."

"There'd better be," Peyton interjected, "because your parents need other grandchildren to keep them from spoiling Ariana."

Alexis turned her attention to Peyton. "So Ariana's

your only child?"

"Yes," Peyton replied. "She's our special angel."

"She is adorable."

"We didn't want her to be an only child, but sometimes things work out differently than you expect." Peyton's gaze drifted off and Alexis felt a rush of sympathy.

"I know exactly what you mean," she said.

Peyton's eyes darted back to her guest. "Do you?" she asked, searching Alexis's face.

"I do."

Peyton smiled vaguely. "Certain times of year bring it all back. The possibilities. The could-have-beens, but then I hug my Ariana and I feel so grateful."

Alexis nodded sympathetically and found herself relieved to have someone who understood and was willing to share. Despite her years abroad, she didn't have that in London. Even with Mark's support, it had been a lonely time for her. The second time, even he wasn't around to offer his support. Those were dark times that Alexis was desperate to move on from.

Tyler listened with half an ear, knowing that he'd missed a critical piece of information. Something had passed between the women and he couldn't quite figure out what it was.

Despite that somber exchange, the rest of the evening passed quickly, with good food and better conversation. Alexis enjoyed herself immensely and joined in the cheering when Tyler appeared with his guitar on the patio.

He played all the silly requests that were thrown his way, including a naughty version of Rudolph the Red-Nosed Reindeer that Alexis had never heard before.

When she could no longer fight the fatigue that plagued her, she thanked the Keelers for a lovely evening and Tyler offered to walk her out.

"Don't be a stranger," Peyton told her. "We'd love to see you again before you go back to London."

"That would be nice," Alexis said and realized that she meant it.

She retrieved her wrap from inside and shivered when she felt Tyler's hand on the small of her back. Outside, most of the golf carts had disappeared.

"It's late," Tyler said. "Let me ride home with you and I'll walk from there."

"Tyler," she objected. "It's perfectly safe."

"I know. I just want more time with you."

Without warning, he pulled her in for a deep, lingering kiss. When he finally released her, he took a tentative step back.

"Was that okay?"

"The kiss itself or the fact that it happened?" she asked, peering up at him.

"I hope the kiss itself was more than okay," he said.

"It was all more than okay," she told him, her stomach performing somersaults.

In an instant, his lips were back on hers and, this time, Alexis responded in a way that removed all doubt. His lips felt better than she'd imagined. She melted against his chest as he wrapped his strong arms around her. Tyler stirred feelings in her that she'd thought were dead and buried. Now it seemed they merely had been dormant.

"I've been waiting a very long time for that kiss," he murmured.

"So Betsy was telling the truth?" And basically everyone at the party, she almost added, but didn't want to embarrass him.

He cocked his head. "Depends on what Betsy said."

"That you may have had a teeny crush on me in high school." She felt embarrassed saying it aloud to him.

"Not true," he said and watched with satisfaction as her shoulders drooped the slightest bit. Then he whispered in her ear, "It was way bigger than teeny."

"In that case, I'm glad you're so patient," Alexis whispered back.

"It's one of my many skills," Tyler told her.

He kissed her again, his tongue darting around her mouth, teasing her. He moved a hand to the back of her head as they continued to taste each other. Her thick, brown hair was as smooth and silky as he'd imagined it. He longed to lose himself in her completely. As his fingers caressed her bare neck, she clutched his back, feeling the muscles beneath his shirt. Her heartbeat accelerated and her entire body hummed with electricity.

Tyler's breathing grew ragged as the urgency of his kisses intensified. His fingers danced their way inside her deep neckline. Musician's fingers, Alexis thought to herself as she felt his hand slip up and under her silky bra. Desire pulsed through her, but she managed to pull herself together. As good as she felt, she wasn't ready for more. Gently, she covered his nimble fingers with her hand.

He pressed his forehead lightly against hers. "Sorry," he said. "It's like all my Christmases coming at once. I can't wait to unwrap you."

"Tyler, I can't rush into anything," she said softly.

"I've waited this long," Tyler said, flashing his trademark dimple. "What's another decade or two?"

She released his hand and adjusted her dress, embarrassed by her display of public affection. How did he work his way under her skin like that? It wasn't her style to engage in hot and heavy make out sessions on someone's front lawn.

His blue eyes twinkled and she fought the urge to pull him in for another kiss.

"My life is complicated," she said.

"I'm not, so whenever you feel like living the simple life, reach out to me. I'll be waiting for you."

He bent to kiss her again and, for once, her mind quieted and she thought of nothing except the feel of Tyler's lips on hers, and how good it felt to be held.

Chapter Twelve

Alexis and Tilly rolled meatballs at the kitchen table, using a recipe that Alexis had learned from her mother-in-law. She was glad that her mother wasn't too territorial in the kitchen and seemed eager to employ some of her daughter's suggestions.

As Tilly chattered away about various neighbors, Alexis's mind drifted to her incredible kiss with Tyler. He was working until five and had invited her to Gatsby's to watch him play again later in the evening. She felt like a giddy teenager, itching to see him again.

"I guess you're not very interested in Harry Weyburn's gall bladder surgery," Tilly remarked.

"Not in any lifetime."

Tilly stopped rolling. "Then why don't you talk to me about something?"

"Like what?"

"Oh, I don't know. Your life. Tell me about my adult daughter, Alexis." She paused. "Tell me about your husband. What's his name?"

"Mark." Alexis cleared her throat. "A good, decent man."

"Did you leave him?"

"No, I didn't leave him." Alexis quickly grew annoyed when she saw her mother's look of surprise. "Is that so shocking?"

"You left us," her mother said quietly. "Why wouldn't you leave him?"

Alexis stopped rolling and met her mother's steady gaze. "I didn't leave him," she repeated.

"Are you going back to London then?" her mother asked.

"I haven't decided what I'm doing next."

"Really? Because of Tyler Barnes?"

Now it was Alexis's turn to be surprised. "Damn Betsy," she hissed.

"Don't blame your sister. Everyone on the island has seen you two together."

"Tyler is…" She started to say just a friend, but that no longer seemed true. "Tyler is aware that there are obstacles."

"Well, we both know you're quite capable of overcoming obstacles, if you really want to."

"I used to think so," Alexis said.

Tilly finished the last meatball and slid the tray into the oven. "But not anymore?"

Alexis didn't want to keep her secrets anymore. She was doing the same thing to her mother that she accused her mother of doing to her. She was demanding to be known and understood, yet withholding the very information that would allow that to happen. It was time to undo some of the damage.

"Mark and I wanted children, but I had two miscarriages," Alexis said. "The first one made it to the second trimester, but I lost the second one at ten weeks."

Tilly's shoulders slackened. "Oh, honey, I'm so sorry."

"Mark was excited to start a family. He used to research everything from prenatal vitamins to the safest car seat. He was so smart, in-house counsel for a big company. He was a kind, loving man, a wonderful husband, and he would've been a great dad."

Tilly's eyes filled with tears. "So what happened?" she gently prodded.

Alexis took a deep breath and told her story.

Alexis hurried into the grand lobby from outside. Bright sunshine burst through the glass doors and windows. She'd just finished presenting to a huge, prospective client and the meeting had gone well. Now all she needed to do was grab her bag from her office and head to the airport where Mark was waiting, probably cursing her under his breath for being late yet again.

As she passed by the front desk, the receptionist gave a polite wave to get her attention. "Mrs. Steamer, you have an urgent message from your secretary."

Alexis wrinkled her nose. "I'm heading up there now."

The receptionist lowered her voice. "They've left several voicemails on your mobile as well."

Alexis fished through her bag for her cell phone. She always kept it turned off during presentations and client meetings.

"Thank you," she said blankly. What was so urgent? She did a mental check of all her current matters and couldn't conjure up any potential disasters. She was only eight weeks pregnant and had recently had her first doctor's appointment, but there was no reason for them to call. They were going to monitor her pregnancy closely because of her previous miscarriage, that was all.

She took the elevator up to her office to listen to her messages in private. Magda, her secretary, wasn't at her desk so Alexis went straight into her office and closed the door. When she heard the sound of her mother-in-law's fractured voice, a shiver ran down her spine.

"It's Mark, Alexis. Please ring me when you get this."

Alexis felt her stomach turn inside out. How could it be Mark? He was sitting in the airport lounge. She dialed Moira's number and waited anxiously. Thankfully, Moira picked up on the first ring.

"What happened?" Alexis asked without saying hello.

"There was an accident on the motorway," Moira began, then stopped, unable to continue.

"But that doesn't make sense. He's already at the airport," Alexis said.

Donald's voice came on next. "He left the airport to come back for you. A lorry overturned on the motorway." He sucked in a deep breath. "They said it was quick."

"But it's our anniversary," she said, as though bad

things didn't happen to people on their anniversary.

"I know," said Donald as she heard Moira's sobs break out in the background.

Alexis didn't know what to say, so she hung up the phone without saying anything. She stared at her reflection in the glass pane of her oversized window. The moment didn't seem real.

The worst day of her life had come without warning, without fanfare; the day even had the nerve to be sunny. She spent the rest of the day sobbing and vomiting on the floor of the office bathroom until Magda finally appeared in the doorway with Hal.

Hal collected her from the bathroom and took her home. She slept on the sofa that night, unwilling to sleep in their bed without Mark. She went without food the next day, until she remembered the baby growing inside her and forced herself to eat a bowl of oatmeal with sliced banana. Mark would want her to eat sensibly for the baby.

Since Donald and Moira were over an hour away and not fully functional, Alexis knew the funeral would be left to her. As ideal as they were in so many ways, Alexis realized that the Steamers were not good when things went bad. They were fair weather people. Alexis, on the other hand, was a MacAdams from Mangrove Island. A place of disappointments and tough love. She didn't dissolve when things didn't go well; she toughened up.

Hundreds of people attended the funeral. Alexis didn't know half of them. People who worked with Mark. Friends of the Steamers. Alexis had Mark dressed in a tasteful Armani suit with his favorite red tie. Alexis stood in the foreground with the Steamers beside her. She opted to forgo the obligatory dark sunglasses, staring down at the casket with clear, dry eyes.

A week after the funeral, Alexis began to bleed uncontrollably and she took herself to the hospital where she received the last of her bad news. Mark was dead and now the only part of him that remained was gone, too.

When she finished her story, Alexis wept in earnest. This was the first time she'd recounted the awful events in such detail. Even her therapist hadn't wrangled the whole story out of her. Difficult didn't begin to describe it.

Tilly's tears flowed freely. She wrapped her daughter in her arms as Alexis tried to calm herself.

"The worst part is, I went straight back to work like nothing happened," Alexis said through sobs. "I was too busy bringing in clients to be with my husband and then I carried on working until I'd lost everything." She spit the word 'working' like it burned her tongue.

"None of it was your fault, Alexis." Tilly stroked her daughter's hair.

"I should've been with him. He was coming back for me because I wasn't where I belonged, with him. After he died, I thought I'd be strong enough to hold myself together for the baby." She stifled another sob. "But I wasn't."

Tilly finally understood. As hard as it was to hear, the truth gave her a sense of peace. "When did all this happen?"

"About eighteen months ago. I thought it was best to keep my routine going afterward, to stay sane, but the firm finally asked me to take a leave of absence. I guess I wasn't able to keep up. I spent a lot of time staring out the window at grey skies. It was depressing everybody."

"Alexis, I'm so sorry." Her mother cupped her chin. "It's a terrible loss, but believe me when I tell you that you are strong." She looked her daughter in the eye. "And I don't think that's only my perception. If you really want to, you'll find a way to stop blaming yourself and live your life. Mark would want that."

Alexis slumped into Tilly's arms, feeling unburdened, and allowed herself to be comforted by her mother for the first time since childhood.

Chapter Thirteen

It was the night of the electricians' union Christmas party so Alexis was the adult in charge at Betsy's house, attempting to earn her aunt stripes. Her nephews sat on the floor in the family room while Tyler played B-I-N-G-O on his guitar.

"And Bingo was his name, oh!" Tyler gave one last exaggerated stroke of the strings and the pint-sized audience clapped wildly.

"Okay, I think Tyler the Guitar Hero deserves a break," Alexis said.

The boys moaned in protest as Tyler followed Alexis into the kitchen. On his way, he saw Brian head for the guitar and gave him a mock threatening look. No one touched the guitar, no matter how cute. Brian shrank back to his seat on the floor.

"Sorry, but they're not big tippers," Alexis joked as they stood in the kitchen.

"It's not cash I'm interested in, little lady." He gave her a meaningful look and she shifted her gaze away, moving to the cabinet to pull out two glasses. She wanted him to focus on something else, especially while they were babysitting. His attention was both exhilarating and frightening.

"How about I serve you a drink for a change?" she asked.

As always, he took her brush off in stride. "I'd like that."

Tyler settled onto a stool while Alexis poured the wine.

"So I've been giving it some thought," he told her, "and it sounds to me like you should quit your job."

"Is that so?"

"You should be doing something you love every single day. Feeding your soul instead of filling your day."

"But I'm a good lawyer." Despite her leave of absence from the firm, Alexis hadn't lost faith in her abilities. It was the one area of her life where she'd never let anybody down.

"So be a different kind of lawyer," Tyler suggested.

"You think I should be a bad lawyer?" she asked playfully.

"I'll bet you couldn't if you tried," he said. "Why not work for a non-profit or be an immigration lawyer? There must be some type of law that would fulfill you."

Owen raced in, unaware of the grown-up conversation taking place. Alexis nearly exhaled with relief, grateful for the interruption.

"The natives are getting breathless!" he gasped.

"You mean restless," Alexis corrected him with a smile.

"Can we have one more song before bedtime, pleeeeease?" He flashed a toothy grin and batted his long eyelashes at them.

Tyler couldn't resist. "Okay then, one more song."

"Hooray!" Owen hustled out of the room ahead of them to tell the others.

"Pushover," Alexis teased and Tyler pinched her bottom in retaliation. "Hey, hands to yourself."

"I'm trying my best," he said, giving her an innocent look. He sauntered back into the family room and called out, "Who likes Rudolph the Red-Nosed Reindeer?"

"The nice version," she hissed behind him.

Once the boys were finally asleep, Alexis and Tyler sat comfortably on the couch, watching A Christmas Carol in the family room. The lights were dimmed and the tree lights twinkled happily in the background.

"So do you think you'll ever write poems again?" asked Tyler. "Maybe we could collaborate."

"What makes you think I stopped? Maybe I've been filling notebooks and stuffing them under my mattress for years."

"Oh, you stopped," he said knowingly. "Maybe you dabbled a little in college, but I'll bet you never wrote anything after that."

"When did you decide all that, Agatha Christie?"

"That first night you came into the bar."

She sighed and leaned her head on his shoulder. "You're right. I gave up that part of myself a long time ago."

"The poet's still in there, you know." He patted his own chest. "Takes one to know one. You should release the hounds. If you write as well as you kiss, you could be the next Maya Angelou."

She covered her face with her hands, embarrassed by his casual reference to their make out session. "Tyler," she protested.

"What's the matter? Alexis, you have nothing to be embarrassed about, believe me. The way you tilted your head at just the right angle. Your tongue was like a hot, wet…"

Her face grew hot. "Tyler, if you say another word on the subject, so help me God, that tree will find its way up your…"

He leapt away from her, grinning mischievously. "Your lips were like red rose petals glistening with dew. I've never experienced a kiss like that in my life."

Alexis couldn't resist a smile. "You're a lucky man, Tyler Barnes."

Tyler eyed her. "I could be luckier."

"And persistent."

He dropped back down beside her and covered her hand with his. "I do get a rise out of watching you squirm." And out of everything else you do, he wanted to add.

"So glad you find me entertaining."

They sat in mutual silence for a moment, enjoying the ambience.

"Do you think this is what it would be like?" he asked.

"What?"

"Having kids."

Alexis stared into her lap. Although she'd told her mother the whole dreadful story, she wasn't ready to confide in Tyler, partly because her emotions were still too raw and partly because she feared his reaction. He stirred such positive feelings in her; she didn't want to risk losing that.

"I don't know," she finally whispered.

"For what it's worth, I think you'd make a great mom. These kids adore you."

As much as it pained her, Alexis gave him a polite smile and uttered the only words she could manage. "Thank you."

The next evening, Alexis stood in her room and deliberated over her outfit for Tyler's annual holiday performance at Gatsby's. She didn't think it counted as a date, since he'd be on stage and she'd be nursing a drink on her own. At this point, though, it was hard to pretend they weren't dating. Once constant companionship progressed to kissing and groping, then it became something else entirely. Thankfully, he seemed to understand that she needed to move at her own pace.

Alexis finally chose jeans and a plum-colored top with a deep v-neck. She glammed it up with diamond stud earrings and a silver bracelet. Alexis couldn't remember a period in her life when she spent so much time choosing clothes to wear. It felt frivolous and, more importantly, fun. When she was finally ready to go, she inspected her reflection in the mirror and was pleased with the results.

"My parents are here tonight," Tyler stated when she arrived. "They'd love to meet you."

Alexis felt her chest tighten. "They're not here for me, are they?"

He laughed. "Wow. I've given you quite the ego, haven't I?" He placed a hand on either of her shoulders and looked into her eyes. "Rest assured, Alexis, as lovely as you are, they're here to see me, their son."

Alexis wanted to melt into the floor. What was wrong with her? Naturally, they were here to enjoy their son's music.

"Having said that," he told her with an impish grin, "would it be too much to ask that you sit with them?"

Alexis hesitated. "I'm not so great with parents."

He put his arm across her shoulder and she instantly relaxed. "Hey, they're not your parents. Just meet them. If they scare you off, then sit somewhere else."

He guided Alexis to an older couple in the far corner of the room.

"Mom, Dad, this is Alexis MacAdams."

"Call me Trey," said Tyler's dad. "And this is Patty."

"Nice to meet you," Alexis said.

"MacAdams," Trey said, rubbing his grey beard. "Does your mother work for Morris?"

"For many years," Alexis said.

"He's our lawyer," Trey said. "Did our wills and some

other personal business."

"Alexis is a lawyer, too," Tyler told them.

Trey smacked his knee. "Gonna give Morris a run for his money, huh? The old geezer could use some youthful competition." He laughed heartily.

"No, I don't live here," Alexis corrected him. "I've been working in London."

Trey whistled. "Smart and pretty with international credentials. I like it." He winked at Tyler.

"Don't mind my husband," Patty chimed in. "He's been eager to see his son settled down for quite some time now. He sees every pretty woman as a potential daughter-in-law."

"Like you don't," Tyler said to his mother good-naturedly.

She fluffed his hair. "I'm a patient woman."

"Must be where I get it," said Tyler. He glanced over his shoulder. "Showtime." He gave his mother a peck on the cheek.

"Alexis, will you join us?" asked Patty.

"She will because I've already asked that her drink be sent to this table." Tyler gave her an unexpected kiss on the lips before he bounced toward the stage.

"I hope I'm not interrupting," Alexis said sheepishly. She fervently hoped his parents had missed the lip lock.

"We have more than enough alone time together," Patty said with a wry smile. "Sometimes it's nice to have a little distraction."

Trey threw a muscled arm around his wife and pulled

her closer. "Nothing can distract me from you, Patty. Don't you know that by now?" He kissed her cheek roughly and Alexis couldn't help but laugh.

Oddly, they reminded her of Mark's parents, minus the English demeanor. She decided it must be what a happy couple looks like.

She'd met the Steamers for the first time at Amaya, an Indian restaurant that Mark's parents enjoyed whenever they were in London. They were a well-dressed and relaxed couple, the kind of couple who did a lot of socializing together. Polar opposites of Alexis's parents.

"I cannot believe you've never had a curry before," Moira had commented.

"My family wasn't big on foreign cuisine. Once when I was seven, we went for Chinese in Fort Myers."

"Once? When you were seven?" Donald had been aghast. Mark had been raised on international cuisine. From sushi to curry to fish and chips. It was all comfort food to him.

Alexis shrugged. "My father kept insisting there was cat hidden somewhere in the menu and making incoherent references to the Korean war."

Mark's father perked up at the mention of war. "Surely, your father is too young to have served in Korea."

"The only thing my father served was beer to himself after work, when my mother wasn't home to fetch it for him."

They all laughed and shook their heads in disbelief.

Mark's mother smiled indulgently at her son. "I think

Mark enjoyed his first curry in the womb. I had to have one every Friday. Donald would bring it home to me after work. It was worse than a craving."

Donald patted his wife's hand at the memory and they shared a nostalgic smile. The gesture caught Alexis's attention because she couldn't recall a single time that her father and mother had ever exchanged loving smiles like that.

Hand-in-hand, Alexis and Mark strolled back to their flat from the restaurant.

"Have your parents always been like this?" she asked.

Mark's face reddened. "Oh God, what did they say when I was in the loo?"

"No, no. They're great. You're so lucky."

Mark gave her a squeeze. "That dinner conversation was the most I've ever heard you say about your parents. You never talk about them."

"No, I don't."

"Do they even know about me?" he asked softly.

Alexis didn't want him to think he was unimportant, but she also didn't want him to think that she was the type of person who didn't speak to her family.

"Would it change anything between us either way?" she asked.

"Of course not."

"Good." Inwardly, she was relieved.

"Well, my parents agree with me," he said.

"About what?"

"That I couldn't have chosen a better partner."

"They don't care that I don't want to sew on your lost buttons or have dinner on the table for you precisely at six?"

"No. Besides, we're lawyers. We're never home by six." He stopped to kiss her firmly. "We love each other. Besides, my mum taught me to cook when I was young and she's teaching you to bake. Between us, we'll have all our meals covered."

"And the buttons can just sew buttons."

"Indeed."

He moved a stray hair from her face, drinking her in.

"What?" she asked.

"I just want to remember this moment. Remember how much I love you."

She kissed him back. "That's sweet and completely unnecessary. I'll never let you forget how much you love me."

Shaking off the memory, Alexis snapped back to the present as the waitress brought her a whiskey. She thanked the girl and offered to pay, but the waitress waved her off and disappeared into the crowd. Her gaze shifted to Tyler as he sat onstage looking completely at ease. He truly loved playing live music and it showed. In that moment, Alexis envied him.

People immediately started calling out song titles. When the bartender demanded White Christmas, everyone started cheering.

"In a holiday mood, are we?" he asked the crowd. They

responded with fierce clapping. "All right then. Let's sing it since, as long as we're on Mangrove Island for Christmas, we have no chance of actually seeing one."

The audience laughed. Trey and Patty were beaming with pride. Everyone was cheerful and Alexis embraced the positive energy swirling through the room.

Tyler began to pluck the strings and his deep, melodic voice filled the room. His was a slow, beautiful rendition of the song and Alexis noticed that several people were moved to tears, including Trey and Patty. When he finished, the crowd sat in awed silence.

"This next song is one I wrote a long time ago, but it's always held a special place in my heart. It's called Mermaid's Kiss."

Alexis listened to the words of the ballad about a boy who meets a mermaid while out at sea and falls in love with her. He manages one kiss before she disappears beneath the waves, never to be seen again. The boy grows into a man and lives out the rest of his days, dreaming of the mermaid and their single kiss.

It was a stirring, wistful song and Alexis was amazed by the complexity of emotions Tyler could bring to a simple song like Mermaid's Kiss. He was even more talented than she'd first thought.

The patrons gave him a standing ovation at the end of it and Alexis thought that even Tyler looked a little teary-eyed.

"I don't know how he'll top that one," Alexis whispered to Patty.

Patty sighed. "He hasn't played that song in years. It's one of my favorites." She pressed a hand to her heart. "I've always been proud to have raised a son who's in touch with his emotions. I feel like I did something right."

"You did a lot of things right," Alexis told her as Tyler began his next song.

Alexis recognized the chords instantly. Yesterday by The Beatles. His soulful version of the song was so heartbreaking that Alexis found herself wiping away tears with her beverage napkin. Embarrassed by her response, she excused herself and went to the restroom.

Thankfully, no one was in there and Alexis closed herself inside a stall and cried in earnest. The tears cascaded down her cheeks and she grabbed a handful of toilet paper to wipe away the evidence. She cried for Mark; she cried for her unborn children. She cried for futures that would never be, hers included. She had been a wife and nearly a mother and now she was neither. Faint strands of the song still echoed in the stall and Alexis pressed her cheek to the cool wall and let the music engulf her. She stayed there until the song finished and she was sure that she could keep it together. She splashed cold water on her face and blew her nose one last time for good measure. Inspecting her face in the mirror, she could see flushed cheeks and pink eyes, but in the dim lights of Gatsby's, she'd probably get by. She reapplied her lipstick and practiced her smile before returning to the table.

"That was beautiful, wasn't it?" Alexis said to his parents as she seated herself.

Patty's hand clutched her heart. "I've never heard him sing that one before. It was amazing."

"He sure got all the talent in our family," Trey said approvingly.

"And the looks," added Patty.

"Oh, come on. Have you two looked in a mirror lately?" Patty and Trey Barnes were a good-looking couple, period. Alexis didn't think anyone could argue with that.

Patty blushed and Trey smiled at his wife. "It's all down to a love of family, music, and the great outdoors."

"Sounds like an ideal combination," said Alexis and turned her attention back to the stage as Tyler geared up for another song.

He played two more of his original songs and ended with Silver Bells, a Christmas crowd pleaser. By the end of the evening, Alexis found her spirits gently lifted. She'd cried more in the past few days than in the months following the accident. It was as though the island was determined to cleanse her soul.

Chapter Fourteen

Alexis studied herself in the mirror and noticed that she looked a bit fleshier than she had back in London. She was relieved that her appetite finally seemed to be returning. Alexis suspected that it was due to more than just good island food.

Tyler had invited her to spend Christmas Eve with him since she planned to spend Christmas Day with her family. He claimed to have something special planned but wouldn't divulge any details. Alexis decided to play it safe with her outfit. She wore black, slim fit jeans and a white silk top with silver hoop earrings. No matter what the evening involved, she figured she would be sartorially appropriate. He seemed so enthusiastic about his secret plan that Alexis, who generally wasn't fond of surprises, couldn't help but feel slightly giddy. It was part of his charm, she realized, that he could wrangle giddiness out of her.

Tyler texted her at seven to say that he was out front. Alexis chuckled to herself. She felt like a teenager sneaking out to meet her boyfriend. Even though she'd spent a lovely evening with his parents at Gatsby's, she wasn't ready for Tyler to endure hers. She was still rebuilding those relationships and she didn't feel comfortable throwing Tyler into the mix. He seemed to respect her feelings on the subject.

Alexis popped her head into the family room to say goodnight to her parents. Her father was snoring in front of a game show she didn't recognize while her mother sat beside a stockpile of presents, both wrapped and unwrapped. Tilly removed her earphones when she noticed Alexis in the doorway.

"What are you listening to?" Alexis asked.

"My Christmas favorites. Nat King Cole, Bing Crosby. Betsy bought me an iPod a few years ago and I use it when your father doesn't want to be distracted by music."

"I think you mean woken up," Alexis said, gesturing to her snoozing father.

Tilly smirked. "He's always tired anymore. I'm starting to think maybe you were right about retirement."

"So how's that elf workshop going?" asked Alexis.

"Almost finished," her mother replied with a grateful sigh. "It was easier when I just had two girls to wrap for. Add three boys and a son-in-law and I'm pooped."

"They look really nice," Alexis told her, admiring the pristine creases and perfect red bows.

"Thank you. Do you need to borrow anything? Scissors?"

"I've taken care of it, thanks."

"So where are you off to on Christmas Eve?"

Alexis felt a pang of guilt, leaving her mother alone with a sleeping father to go enjoy herself elsewhere. "Tyler Barnes invited me out."

"Naturally."

"It's been good for me, I think, to reconnect with old friends." Never mind that he wasn't technically an old friend. "Tyler's waiting, so I should go. Goodnight."

She carried on out the front door before any further questions were asked. Tyler stood outside, looking gorgeous in a blue crew neck top that highlighted his eyes and tight, dark jeans. Alexis wondered what was inside the black bag slung over his shoulder.

He whistled appreciatively as she approached him. "More beautiful by the day."

She blushed. "You don't look too bad yourself."

"I try not to disappoint. Wouldn't want you to forget me again."

"No golf cart?" Alexis queried.

"We're bipeds tonight, my lady."

She tried to think where they'd be going within walking distance and came up empty. She was glad that she chose flat shoes, a fact that Tyler noticed immediately.

"You're picking up my casual vibe," he said, nodding toward her aqua flip-flops. "I like it."

"I've realized there's something soothing about the sound of flip-flops," she admitted. "Certainly better than getting my heels stuck in the sand."

His eyes widened. "Oh, so you think we're headed to

the beach. Well, smart girl, not so smart after all." He held out his arm and she looped her arm through his.

"Okay, you've outwitted me, Barnes. Are we going to raid Jo's Convenience Store? Lowry's? Because there aren't many places I can think of nearby."

"How quickly we forget," he said, clucking his tongue with disappointment.

The stars shone brightly against a black sky as they walked to the end of her road and turned right. When he reached for her hand, a jolt of electricity coursed through her. She felt the rough skin on his fingers from years of playing guitar and instinctively wanted to bring them to her lips and kiss each one, but she withstood the urge. Alexis noticed a couple of dog walkers coming toward them, illuminated by the streetlights.

"God, I had such a flashback of passing all the dogs on my way to school every morning. I guess that dog park is still there."

She glanced at Tyler and noticed his sly smile. "Are we going to the dog park?" she asked in disbelief.

He shook his head and could hardly contain his laughter. "Not quite."

As soon as she realized their destination, she felt like an idiot. School. He was literally taking her back to high school.

"You can't be serious," she said.

"C'mon," he urged her. "It'll be fun. I think you need to replace some of those twisted memories of yours with better ones."

He squeezed her hand as they carried on walking toward the school. Alexis surveyed the neighborhood on the way.

"Everything looks the same."

"Places like this don't change very much," he said. "You don't fix what isn't broken."

"You should work for the tourist board."

"I'd happily write them a catchy jingle for their commercials. For free."

Alexis laughed. "You're nuts. I've never known anyone so in love with their hometown."

"Then clearly you haven't met anyone from Pittsburgh." He glanced over the fence. "There she blows. The mother ship."

Alexis stopped and stared at her past. Woodrow Wilson High School. The building looked so small now, apart from a wing she didn't recognize.

"Did they add on to it?"

"Yep. Population boom. It wasn't like they were going to build another high school on the island."

Alexis studied the grounds and the lot for golf carts. It was funny to think of it now, a school where kids rode golf carts instead of a bus or a car. How many people could say that?

"Do you remember Mr. Bodner?" she asked suddenly, having a sudden vision of her old soccer coach.

"He's retired," Tyler told her. "Comes into The Blue Heron sometimes. His wife died a few years ago, but he's been dating Mindy Larkin's grandma so he's not lonely."

"That's a shame about his wife. I remember her. She was sweet."

"Breast cancer." He paused. "She threw a party and made sure to invite all of Mr. Bodner's friends so that he was forced to reconnect with people before she died. She was worried about him becoming the town hermit."

"No man is an island, even if he lives on one," Alexis said.

"I believe that." He fixed his gaze on her. "Do you?"

Alexis fell silent. The truth was that she did believe it, but she felt ill-equipped to build the necessary bridges.

"Let's see if we can get inside," Tyler suggested, breaking into a sprint.

Alexis stumbled after him in her flip-flops. "Tyler, wait!"

She watched as his long, lean frame grew smaller. When she finally caught up to him, he was standing at the top of the front steps, tapping his foot with mock impatience. She, on the other hand, was doubled over with a pain in her side and struggling to catch her breath.

"Someone's gone a bit soft," he said. "I thought city people were all gym obsessed."

"I never had time for the gym," she told him. "Too many billable hours."

"Must be genetics then," he said, admiring her figure. "See, your parents were good for something, after all."

She blushed, suddenly feeling self-conscious. "How are we getting in?" she asked, shifting the focus away from her body.

He produced a key. "I have friends in high places."

She cocked her head. "Let me guess, the janitor drinks at your bar."

Tyler grinned. "He does, but he also plays poker with me."

"High places, indeed."

Tyler turned the key in the lock and swung the door open with dramatic flair. He gestured for her to go first. Hesitantly, Alexis walked into the darkness. She felt Tyler's hand move to the small of her back and felt that electric current spread throughout her body. He filled the space behind her and closed the door. She couldn't see her hand in front of her face.

"These lights are here somewhere," he said, feeling along the wall.

Suddenly, Alexis saw a small circle of light appear beside her.

"What's that?" she asked with a start.

"Flashlight app." He swirled it around in the darkness. "Oooh, scary."

"You're ridiculous," she said, laughing.

"Ridiculously sexy." With that, the hallway lights were switched on and Alexis was transported back to high school.

"Holy crap," she breathed, taking in the entrance hall. She was instantly flooded by memories. "It looks the same."

"It does," he agreed.

"Have you been here since graduation?" she asked.

"I have. Sometimes they have evening classes here or charity events. It's used by the whole community."

"I never thought I'd see it again." She touched the light green walls and wondered which color-blind administrator thought light green was the right color for the school hallways.

"Welcome to Woodrow Wilson High School," Tyler said, imitating a tour guide. "Today you'll be learning how the most unique of humans, the teenager, eats, exercises and learns within these hallowed halls."

"You should've brought your guitar," Alexis said. "A musical guided tour would've been much cooler."

"I didn't want to cheat."

"Cheat?" She shook her head, confused. "What do you mean?"

"If I had strummed my guitar while making you feel seventeen again, your hormones would've raged. You wouldn't have been able to keep your hands off me." He shrugged modestly. "Unfair advantage."

She broke into a wide smile. "You really think the ladies have a thing for musicians, don't you?"

He shrugged. "Years of hard evidence."

She raised an eyebrow. "Hard evidence, eh?"

"Let's start our tour, shall we?" He clasped her hand and began walking toward the gym.

"School dance memories," she said, as they pushed through the double doors. The lights in the gym flickered on automatically.

"You went with that moron, Josh," Tyler grumbled.

Alexis glanced at him in amazement. "Tyler Barnes, are you still jealous of a boy who took me to the prom all those years ago?"

His blue eyes blazed. "Hell, yes."

"Who did you take to the prom?" she asked.

"Shea Marino," he replied.

Alexis bit her lip, trying to summon a memory of Shea Marino. She threw up her hands in frustration. "Not in my mental file."

"Somehow, I'm not surprised. She was quiet and shy, probably the reason I asked her. Plus, we were friends from strings club. I knew she'd say yes."

"A quiet and shy rocker chick, huh? Pretty different from me."

"Shea played the violin. Not quite a rocker chick. She's a music teacher now, in Atlanta. Three kids. A dog. Probably feeds stray cats, too."

Tyler unzipped his bag and handed her a blindfold. "For you."

She took the blindfold and held it at bay. "What am I supposed to do with this?"

"Alexis MacAdams, more vanilla than I realized."

"Nothing wrong with vanilla," she insisted, now worried what Tyler had in store.

"Relax," he said, "it's not what you think." He gestured for her to sit in the first row of the gym bleachers. Then he took the blindfold and placed it over her eyes.

"I guess this is the surprise, then." She heard him rifling through his bag and moving around the gym. Each sound echoed throughout the empty room. "Sounds like it's all under masterful control."

"Ah, that's the beauty of the blindfold. I look better and sound more organized."

"Christ, Barnes. Are you building me the Tower of Babel because need I remind you that God didn't love that token of affection so much?"

"Hey, cut me some slack. I'm trying to do something special before you disappear again."

Alexis stiffened. "I'm not a rabbit in a hat."

"Just keep those pretty peepers covered for one more minute while I finish setting up." He pulled down the large screen behind the basketball backboard and returned to remove her blindfold. "Ta da."

Alexis surveyed the scene. A laptop, a projector, and a large screen were now in view. "So what's playing tonight? Say Anything? Will you be whipping out your boom box at any moment?"

"Steady now. There will be no whipping out of anything...unless you want me to." Tyler wiggled his eyebrows suggestively.

Alexis shot him a warning glance.

"As I suspected. Anyway, times they have a'changed."

Tyler flashed his iPhone. Then he picked up another remote control device. He clicked it and the screen was filled with an image of Alexis. Her high school yearbook photo. Alexis's eyes widened in amazement. Quickly, she covered them.

"Oh my God, are you insane? That photo is hard

enough to take when it's two by three inches."

Tyler laughed, enjoying her discomfort. He clicked again and then played his iPhone. "Now pipe down and enjoy the show. It's the director's cut, complete with musical commentary."

Alexis recognized one of Tyler's songs, Goodbye Girl, as his melodic voice filled the air. The images were all of Alexis. Baby Alexis. Alexis and Betsy at the park. Alexis and her family at the beach. She wore a huge smile in every photo.

"I am going to assume you had some help with this or you have scary skills I would rather not know about."

Tyler expressed an inch with his fingers. Maybe a bit of help.

The photos moved to Alexis in high school. Alexis running a yearbook committee meeting. Alexis on the soccer field, even one where she'd posed with Paige and two other girls. Alexis on the front steps of school, writing in a red notebook. When a more recent photo flashed onscreen of a professional-looking Alexis, she shot him a quizzical look.

Tyler shrugged. "Your LinkedIn profile shot."

The film finished with a photo of Alexis's head superimposed on King Kong's body at the top of the Empire State Building. Without waiting for her disapproving look, Tyler offered, "Your Facebook profile shot."

She crossed her arms and eyed him suspiciously. "You know I'm not on Facebook."

The music faded. Alexis remained fixed on the screen, her mind flooded with all the old images. Tyler turned off the projector and patiently awaited a response.

Emotions flowed through her. "When did you have time for this?" she asked in a small voice.

"You make time for the things you love," he said. Slowly, he traced her jawline with his finger. "And the people."

She gazed up at him, her hazel eyes shining with tears. "Did you write Goodbye Girl about me?"

He nodded. "Years ago. And Mermaid's Kiss. You inspired a lot of my music."

She shook her head in disbelief. "But why me? You didn't know me, not really. What if you only love some high school boy's idea of me?"

He sat down beside her and cupped her chin in his hand. "I am in love with you, Alexis MacAdams, the woman with a hard shell exterior, but a soft, gooey center."

"So, basically, you think I'm a Cadbury egg," she remarked, managing a smile.

"I do love chocolate."

After a brief moment of silence, Alexis decided to take the plunge. Tyler deserved to know the truth and she was ready to tell him.

"I told you I was married," she said and inhaled deeply. "What I didn't tell you, what I couldn't bring myself to say, is that he died."

She stared at the floor as the entire story tumbled out.

Mark's accident on their anniversary, her miscarriages, her inability to make the people in her life a priority. She didn't sob this time, the way she had when she told her mother. This time she felt more nervous than sad, worried what Tyler would think of her. When she finally gathered the courage to look at him, she saw only concern and sadness reflected in his azure eyes.

He squeezed her hand. "I'm glad you told me. I'm sorry you had to go through all that. Nobody deserves that kind of pain."

"But don't you see? I do deserve it. I was a horrible, selfish person and everyone around me suffered as a result. Mark never got to be a father because of me and he certainly didn't get the devoted wife he deserved."

"Doesn't sound that way to me," Tyler said softly. "Sounds like he knew exactly who he married and loved her very much."

"I couldn't even keep his baby," she whispered. "I had a chance to bring a piece of Mark into this world after he died and I couldn't hold on to it. I'm like a black hole."

Tyler wrapped his arms around her and pulled her close. "You have a beautiful, shining soul, Alexis." He kissed her forehead. "And you didn't do anything wrong."

"I feel like I've failed everyone who's ever cared about me."

"You haven't failed me."

He kneeled down in front of her and stroked her cheek, their eyes still on each other. Alexis sat perfectly still, despite the heat radiating from her core. She knew he tasted of salt water and sunshine and she longed to taste him again. Her memory of Mark, however, kept her rooted firmly in place. Alexis didn't want to betray her husband. Her brain told her that she was ridiculous, that Mark would want her to be happy. Her heart, however, beat with caution. As it had taken the brunt of her pain, it seemed uneasy about forming new attachments. On the other hand, she'd found the strength to tell Tyler the truth and he hadn't rejected her. Tyler had described himself as a patient man, and Alexis was starting to believe him.

"You're too good for me, Tyler Barnes," she said.

"I'd like to hear more about Mark, one day when you feel ready," he told her. "Sounds like a good guy. Smart enough to fall in love with you, anyway."

Grateful tears streamed down her cheeks, but she made no attempt to hide them. Tyler reached over and gently wiped one away. She rested her forehead on his, relieved that she kept her secrets no more.

"It's almost a new year, Alexis. Let it be a fresh start."

"Thank you, Tyler," she croaked. "I will try."

"I just want you to remember who you were. Who you still are."

Almost inaudibly she said, "I remember."

"I do have one more token of affection," he said, leaning down to retrieve something from his bag. "And now it seems even more appropriate."

He produced a tall box wrapped in silver paper with a single red ribbon threaded around it. "Merry Christmas, Alexis."

Alexis stared at the gift, dumbfounded. "You bought me a present?"

"It is Christmas Eve and I've brought you back to high school. I owe you something for that, right?" He winked and held out the box.

As she reached out to accept it, she realized her hands were shaking. "Tyler, I'm touched and completely mortified. I didn't get you anything."

"You're with me tonight. That's all I wanted."

Alexis carefully undid the paper and ribbon so as not to rip it. The box was plain white with no hint as to its contents. She opened the lid of the box and saw the unmistakable top of a champagne bottle.

"Tyler! Dom Perignon," she said, pulling out the elegant bottle. "You shouldn't have spent so much."

"Okay, before you feel too guilty, let's not forget I have connections. I don't exactly pay full price, if that helps."

"Should I open it now?"

He placed a hand over the top and shook his head. "Absolutely not. This is for your future." She gave him a quizzical look and he continued. "As much as I like that you don't indulge in overcomplicated cocktails, my Christmas wish is to see you branch out from the whiskey. You know who drinks whiskey in regular rotation? Sad people. Believe me, I've tended enough bar to know it's a fact. And I don't want you to be sad anymore, Alexis. I want to see you drinking champagne and laughing when the fizz hits your nose."

Alexis hugged the bottle of champagne to her body.

"Thank you, Tyler. You seem to know what I need better than I do."

"I just want to lay the foundation for you to move on to happier drinks, whenever you feel ready."

Alexis gazed into his devoted blue eyes and an intense desire for him overcame her. She carefully placed the bottle on the floor beside her.

"So what kind of music do you have on that iPhone?" she asked.

"The good kind, obviously."

"Why don't we dance? Josh was a terrible dancer. I'd like to see how you measure up."

He wasted no time in hustling over to his phone to scroll through his playlist. He hit play and spun around to see Alexis right behind him. She stepped into his embrace as the first notes of Bittersweet Symphony bounced off the gym walls.

"The Verve, right?" she asked.

He nodded and she saw that familiar longing in his eyes. She couldn't resist his pull as he leaned down to kiss her tenderly on the lips. Her stomach fluttered in response and she pressed herself against his broad chest. She felt proof of his arousal as his kisses intensified. As his tongue probed her mouth, she felt herself relaxing, opening herself to him.

"So you liked my gifts?" he murmured. His lips moved to her ear and then down her neck until her whole body tingled with need. He wanted to feel every inch of her, not just her shoulders or her neck. All of her.

"Uh-huh." She ran a hand down his chest and felt the tightness of his abs beneath his shirt. When his hand slipped under her silk top, she moaned at his touch on her bare skin.

"So Shea Marino. Did she kiss you?" Alexis asked.

"No, I didn't want her to kiss me." He brought his lips back to hers. "I only wanted you."

Chapter Fifteen

The next morning Alexis opened her eyes and stared at the blank ceiling. Christmas Day. She rolled onto her side and squeezed her eyes shut again, tightening her fingers on the sheet. For a brief moment, she experienced her knee-jerk reaction of misery, until she remembered the night before. Tyler. She relaxed her grip on the sheets and played the evening over in her mind. Even though he'd slowed things down in the school gym after a hot and heavy petting session, she knew it was for her benefit and not because he wanted to. Tyler Barnes was a gentleman, no one could argue with that. And his gift. She glanced to the dresser where the bottle of champagne sat, patiently waiting. Like Tyler. Although she wasn't ready to pop the cork just yet, she appreciated the sentiment. Hope in a bottle. Thanks to Tyler, life was becoming not simply bearable, but enjoyable. She threw back the covers, rejecting her instinct to hide under them.

Last Christmas was horrible. Donald and Moira had invited her to stay with them, but the atmosphere had been grim. Every time she looked at Donald, she saw the man that Mark would never become and, reflected in Moira's eyes, she saw only a mother's grief. Alexis ended up leaving on Boxing Day with a container full of leftover turkey she knew she would never eat.

It had been Moira, however, who planted the seed about a return to Mangrove Island during that Christmas meal. Alexis's heart had been too hard at the time to fully listen, but the suggestion had taken root, and when the firm finally asked her to take a leave of absence, or a sanity break as tactful Hal had called it, she knew where she intended to go. She had loose ends to tidy up between selling the flat and passing on her caseload to eager associates, so it had taken months before she could actually book a flight and commit to the idea. Even though she could have alerted her parents or Betsy to her impending arrival, the truth was that she feared their rejection. In her experience, it was harder to reject someone standing in front of you, so she'd decided to forgo the phone call and email and simply turn up unannounced. The strategy seemed to have paid off, or there was that small possibility that perhaps she'd underestimated her parents' love for her. That they never would have told her not to bother showing up. Feeling heartened, Alexis got out of bed and into the shower.

Once clean and presentable, Alexis made her way downstairs and peeked into the family room. Presents in varied cheerful wrapping paper sat beneath the tree. Her father watched Fox News while slurping a cup of coffee.

"Merry Christmas, Dad."

He glanced up at her, uncertain. "Merry Christmas. Betsy's brood will be here soon for brunch. They always come for Christmas brunch and dinner."

The implication seemed to be that Alexis did not.

"Is Mom in the kitchen?" she asked, brushing off his remark. It was Christmas and she was surrounded by family. She would not be baited into any arguments.

"Where else would she be?"

Her father returned his attention to the television, so she hesitantly moved into the kitchen where her mother's arms and legs were flying in a cooking frenzy.

"Grab me that pan, will you, dear?" Alexis dutifully retrieved the pan from the end of the counter and handed it to her mother. "Once they get here, it's action stations. I try to do as much as I can ahead of time."

"I'll set the table."

"That would be helpful. Thank you."

Alexis began collecting dishes and cutlery for the table.

"I'm making roast beef," Tilly informed her, "but Betsy's bringing a broccoli and cheese quiche. I hope that's okay."

"Perfect, thank you." Alexis was moved by her mother's consideration. If she had refused roast beef as a teen, she was certain her parents would have made her sit at the table until she ate it, however long it took.

"How do you normally spend Christmas?" Tilly asked tentatively.

"I used to spend it with Mark's family."

"This year will be hard for them, then."

"Yes, I suppose so." Alexis knew that the Steamers were spending this Christmas with Mark's aunt and uncle so they wouldn't be alone.

There was a rush of activity at the front door and they realized that Betsy and her clan had arrived. As quick as a flash, Owen materialized in the kitchen.

"Merry Christmas!" he said, bouncing up and down with such force that Alexis wondered how many cookies he managed to sneak before breakfast.

Tilly gave him a hurried kiss on the cheek. "Merry Christmas, dear. Now don't be underfoot."

Owen moved on to Alexis. "Can I help?"

"Sure. Here."

She handed him some forks. He put them on the table and proceeded to make a design with them instead of setting the table. Tilly glanced over.

"Owen, none of your foolishness. Put them by the plates, please."

Owen's small face crumpled. He gathered up the forks and did as he was told.

Alexis leaned over and whispered, "I thought it was a beautiful design."

The little boy beamed at her. They finished the table and Owen took Alexis's hand and dragged her into the family room.

Brian was in the process of picking up each gift and shaking it. He made multiple guesses as to what was inside. Then, in the far corner, he spied a scooter with a big red ribbon on it.

"No way! It's exactly the one I wanted."

Alexis shot her sister an uneasy glance as Brian read the tag.

"It's from Santa!" he announced.

Owen looked puzzled. "Why would Santa leave us presents here? He knows where we live."

"Sometimes Santa makes a mistake, but he can't turn back because he's on a schedule, so he leaves a gift where you're sure to get it," Alexis explained.

"Santa's a genius!" Owen gushed.

"He's not a genius if he makes mistakes, dummy," Brian said.

"Brian, don't call your brother names," Joe said sternly.

Alexis gestured toward the right side of the tree. "Owen, I think he may have left something for you, too."

Owen rushed to the tree and scoured the gifts. He pulled out a book-shaped present. "This one says Owen! Can I open it, Mom?"

Betsy nodded and Owen tore away the paper.

"It has dinosaurs! What does it say?"

Betsy leaned down to read the cover. "I Wonder Why the Dodo is Dead and Other Questions About Extinct and Endangered Animals."

"Awesome!" He hugged the book to his chest and Alexis sighed inwardly, pleased with her purchase. Betsy's expression toward her sister softened.

"Elmo!" Joey cried.

Joey pulled out an Elmo DVD and talking Elmo doll

from under the tree. He started squeezing Elmo's belly and laughing when Elmo talked. Joe beamed, taking pleasure in his son's enjoyment.

"I thought you were going to get me something," Brian said to Alexis.

Alexis ruffled his hair. "I need to get to know you better first so I don't buy you some lame gift. I'll do better next time. When's your birthday?"

"May thirtieth."

"I'll do better May thirtieth then."

Brian gave her a big smile and returned to his scooter.

"Look, Santa left something else here," Alexis said, plucking a small, wrapped box from under the tree and handing it to Betsy.

"Really?" Betsy asked. "Wow, my first adult Christmas gift from Alexis."

"Well, it's not a handmade tree ornament. I hope you're not disappointed."

Betsy laughed, remembering Alexis's efforts at crafting Christmas ornaments out of salt dough and ribbons. "I might still have a few of those."

Betsy reached into her shoulder bag and pulled out a package for Alexis. The wrapping paper was decorated with reindeer and covered in green and red tape.

"I'm going to go out on a limb and guess you had some help wrapping this," Alexis remarked with a smile.

"Where would Santa be without his elves?" Betsy replied as she tore off the wrapping paper. "Oh, Alexis. You shouldn't have."

It was a gift card for Salters, the nicest shop on the island for home décor.

"I didn't want to choose for you," Alexis explained. "I thought we might go together, though, so I can see the type of things you like."

Betsy clasped the gift card to her chest. "Thank you, Alexis. That's a great idea." She sighed. "Yours is so sweet, now I want to do mine over."

Alexis began to unwrap her present. "I'm sure I'll love it." She pulled out a hand painted sign that read 'You And I Are Sisters, Always Remember That If You Fall I Will Pick You Up…After I Finish Laughing.' Alexis snickered.

"I had Debbie Facinelli make it for you. Do you remember her? She graduated with me. She's got a handmade craft shop in Flamingo Key, near Gatsby's."

Alexis admired the sign. "Good for her. Was she the one who painted the principal's golf cart with red hearts and rainbows?"

Betsy lit up. "Yes! He was so impressed with her work that he hired her to paint his daughter's bedroom."

The sisters smiled at the memory.

"I have one more thing for you," Alexis said, pulling out a manila envelope and handing it to her sister.

Betsy opened the envelope and retrieved the papers inside. "Wow, this looks so professional."

"Kinda what I do," Alexis said with a shrug. "It was actually fun working on it."

Betsy scanned the options, her brown eyes lighting up. "Is this for real?"

"Well, I will need hard numbers from your books and a valuation, but I did a little research so that I could come up with a few possibilities." She smiled. "I think you could have your cake shop and eat it, too, if you really want to."

Betsy threw her arms around her sister. "What an awesome Christmas present."

"What is it, babe?" asked Joe from across the room.

"Thanks to my sister, I'm gonna be a mogul."

"A mogul?" Joe echoed. "Sounds expensive."

Betsy rolled her eyes. "I'll tell you about it later." She clutched the papers happily. "I'll read these over as soon as I get some peace and quiet."

"If any of it confuses you, call me or send me a text and I'll explain."

Betsy was more excited about this than the lace teddy Joe had given her earlier that morning. She decided to keep that fact to herself.

Hours later, Betsy's brood was gone but their remnants lingered. Garbage bags full of wrapping paper and ribbons. Cups and dishes. Tilly rested on the couch with a cup of tea, unwilling to tackle the mess around her yet. Greg napped noisily in his chair. Alexis emerged from upstairs and wandered into the kitchen for a drink.

"Tea's already made." Her mother's voice came from behind her.

Tilly handed her a cup and Alexis sat down at the table. A large, wrapped box with a red bow sat in the middle of the table.

"What's this?"

"Your Christmas present."

Alexis looked at her mother. Even though it was Christmas, she wasn't expecting anything. Slowly, she unwrapped the gift to reveal a cardboard box full of papers. She poked through and something looked familiar. Eagerly, she pulled out a red notebook.

"My poetry notebook. I assumed you tossed it years ago."

"No, it's been here all along."

Alexis paged through the notebook, then poked her nose enthusiastically back into the box to see what else Santa had brought. She pulled out an award certificate.

"First prize in the poetry contest junior year."

"They're all there," Tilly told her. "Every award. Every achievement of yours that we apparently don't value or support."

Alexis was almost reduced to tears wading through the papers. Each one held special significance for her.

"I didn't think you cared about this stuff."

"Well, they came from you, dear. They're part of who you are. I never dreamed it would be so many years before I would return them to you."

As Tilly fought back tears, Alexis gently placed a hand on her mother's back.

"We did our best, Alexis," her mother sniffed. "I wish I could've been the kind of mother you wanted, but I'm so glad you're here now."

Seeing her mother on the verge of tears, Alexis felt

horrible. Despite recent evidence to the contrary, the MacAdams family did not produce tears easily. She realized how terribly ungrateful she seemed to her parents. She'd spent so much time feeling aggrieved, a victim of her surroundings, she hadn't considered how her attitude had affected her parents.

"Thank you for this," she said. "It means a lot." She picked up the red notebook and started to read through it from the beginning.

"Why don't you read a few of them to me?" Tilly suggested.

"Really?" She paused. "They're probably awful. What sounded dramatic at sixteen will probably sound ridiculous now."

"I'll take the risk," her mother told her and patted the chair beside her.

Alexis sat down and began to read.

Chapter Sixteen

When Alexis emerged from her bedroom the next morning, she was surprised to see her father already seated at the kitchen table. She checked her watch; it was seven o'clock.

"Are you feeling okay, Dad?" she asked, placing a hand on his shoulder.

"Fit as a fiddle or, in my case, more like a cello. Why?" He picked up a pencil and scribbled something down.

"It's finally a chance to sleep in, yet here you are." Alexis peered over his shoulder to see what he was doing. "A crossword?" she asked in disbelief.

"What's wrong with that?" He pulled the crossword book closer to him, protecting it from her view.

"Nothing. I just don't remember you enjoying crosswords."

"I didn't know I liked them until a few years ago. Joey's school had a fundraiser selling books and I wanted to get something, you know, to show support."

"And you chose a crossword. Interesting." Alexis

retrieved a mug from the cupboard and poured herself a cup of coffee.

"It's not interesting," Greg insisted. "You used to spend hours doing crosswords, if I remember correctly."

"I did." She smirked. "And, as I recall, you used to make fun of me. Told me to learn a real skill, like handling a saw."

"Well, now I can do both. How about you?" His blue eyes twinkled and she knew he was teasing her.

She pulled out a chair and joined him at the table. "No work today, then?"

He shook his head. "I took the whole week off. Merry Christmas."

"Where's Mom?"

"She's sleeping in for a change."

"Good for her. She worked hard yesterday."

"What's a six-letter word for a medicinal tree?" he asked.

"Acacia," she answered after a brief pause.

He filled in the crossword. "Did you know your mother and I have been married for forty years?"

"This year?"

"May."

Alexis sipped her coffee. "Any special plans?"

"I was thinking of taking her on a trip."

Alexis nearly spat out her coffee. Her father was voluntarily planning a trip? "Wow. To where?"

"Thought you might have a recommendation." He completed another answer in the crossword.

She waited for a snide remark about all her fancy travels but none came. "Hot or cold?" she finally asked.

"Not too cold. We're not Eskimos. Not too far, either. I don't want some eight- hour flight over an ocean. No offense."

"None taken. They're not much fun."

"What are your plans for today?" he asked.

"Nothing this morning, but my friend is taking me to Verde Beach later today."

"Nice beach. Peaceful. I like to fish there sometimes."

"I haven't been since ninth grade when we took a class trip to watch the birds."

"Eagles, osprey, heron. You get all sorts there. Protecting that part of the island is something the government actually got right."

A smile tugged at the corners of her mouth. She felt a political rant coming on.

"Your friend is from school, right? Tyler?"

Alexis nodded, surprised once more that he didn't follow his usual verbal path. "He's a really talented musician."

"Been watching him play, huh?" He tapped the pencil on his temple. "An eleven letter word? Oh, c'mon." He pushed the crossword out of reach in annoyance.

She pulled the page toward her to read the clue. "Good one," she said, smiling. "It's portmanteau. I learned that word from a book."

"One of your hundred dollar college books?"

She pushed the crossword back over to him. "Nope.

Through the Looking-Glass by Lewis Carroll. I read it right here when I was a kid."

"Seems I should have been more interested in what you were up to. Do you think Owen would like that book?"

Her face brightened. "I do." She loved that the idea occurred to her father. "I bet he would like it even more if you read it to him."

"Something to consider," he agreed. He then regarded her carefully, as though he was debating something. "You know, your mother and I have a deal."

"What kind of deal?"

"We both want to be cremated without a big service. Just a small get-together back at the house."

Alexis's brow furrowed. "Are you planning to go anytime soon?"

He smiled briefly. "No, but you never know." His eyes flickered to hers and she realized that her father was acknowledging her loss. Obviously, her mother had told him about Mark. Alexis expected that she would; she just didn't expect her father to bring it up. Greg MacAdams was not someone who spoke openly on emotional topics. Political ones, yes. Matters of the heart, no way.

"You have wills, right?" she asked. "Morris wouldn't let Mom get away without it, I imagine."

"We do." He hesitated. "We also have another deal that isn't in our wills."

"You really need everything in writing," she advised. "What is it?"

"Whichever one of us goes first, the other one is free to

go out and find a new partner. No long-term grieving allowed."

Alexis stared at her father. "So if mom dies first, you're supposed to run out and marry the next woman you see?"

He set down his pencil and looked at her. "No. I'm supposed to find someone else who makes me happy, or at least someone whose company I enjoy. Life is too short to spend it alone, Alexis."

"And Mom will do the same?"

"Yes."

"And when did you agree to these terms?" she asked archly.

"Our wedding night, nearly forty years ago. Still haven't changed our minds. We love each other, but one of us can live without the other if that's how it pans out."

"That's romantic," she mumbled.

"No, it isn't, but you know your mother. She likes her lists as much as you do. Helps her feel more in control of things she knows damn well she has no control over."

Alexis bit her lip, her eyes fixed on the tabletop. "And you're okay with that? The idea of her with another man."

"I'll be dead. What do I care?" He shrugged. "Anyway, it wouldn't erase the love she has for me. If I'm not here to make her happy, I sure would like it if someone else could do the job. God knows she deserves it."

Alexis nodded, understanding the words that he'd left unspoken — and you do, too.

He returned his attention to the crossword. "I'm glad you've been able to reconnect with old friends since you've been home. I hear that Tyler is a real nice guy. Good to his folks and his neighbors."

Alexis couldn't resist a small roll of the eyes. "Real subtle, Dad, but thanks." She took her coffee cup and placed it in the sink. "You know what might make Mom happy while you're still alive and kicking? Cleaning up the kitchen once in a while."

He raised a scruffy eyebrow but didn't turn his head. "Have fun at Verde Beach."

Alexis was nervous about meeting Tyler at his house before they went to Verde Beach. He'd made such a good impression so far; she didn't want to discover any bad habits now. Nothing turned her stomach like a dirty bathroom.

The house was a real beach bungalow, painted cottage white with a bright blue door and a green roof. The lawn was neatly manicured with a couple of potted plants beside the porch steps. Charming was the first word that sprang to mind.

As she was about to knock on the door, the whirring sound of a lawn mower caught her attention and she glanced next door to see Tyler zipping along the front of his neighbor's lawn. He waved when he saw her and she raised a confused hand in return. She checked her watch to make sure she had the right time. She did.

He turned off the mower and trotted over to her, sweaty and smelling of freshly cut grass. In Alexis's mind, a lethally sexy combination.

"I'm so sorry," he said, bounding up the steps. "The door's open."

"I can come back later if…"

He cut her off. "No, no. It's my fault. Mrs. Addy needed her yard done and I meant to do it earlier, but inspiration hit this morning and I couldn't get out there until I finished."

He opened the door and held it for her. Alexis stepped inside and casually surveyed the interior.

"Do you have a lawn business, too?" she asked.

"No," he said, closing the door behind them. "Her sons are grown and her husband died a few years ago. She can't manage it on her own."

Alexis took a good look at him. His yellow t-shirt was like a highlighter for his muscles. She pretended not to notice. "That's really kind, Tyler."

He shrugged. "She's my neighbor."

Alexis tried to imagine random acts of kindness between neighbors in London. She nearly laughed out loud. She didn't even know her neighbors' names. When she went from visibly pregnant back to her trim figure without a baby to show for it, no one around them seemed to notice. Even when Mark died, no neighbors paid their respects. They either didn't realize her life had changed forever or they simply didn't care. The thought churned up a bitter taste in her mouth.

"How was Christmas with your parents?" she asked.

"Great. They asked after you."

"That's sweet. Mine was more tolerable than expected."

She shook her head, realizing that it wasn't true. "Actually, it was better than that."

"Glad to hear it." Tyler pulled his top over his head. "I just need to change really fast. I reek of lawn care."

He sprinted down the hall and Alexis heard a drawer open and shut. She admired the artwork on the walls and her gaze lingered over a photo of Tyler and his parents on one of the end tables. They appeared to be on a boat with Tyler and his dad holding up a large tarpon while his mom wrapped a proud arm around her son. Their wide smiles told the story of happy fishermen. Alexis sighed with contentment. Simple pleasures appealed to her more and more each day.

"Is that a silver king?" she called, observing the fish's excessive size and silver scales on the side. It had to be at least six feet long.

"Sure is. One of my dad's proudest moments."

"I can tell."

"That fish had the fighting spirit, no doubt, but I managed to reel her in." He emerged in a clean charcoal-colored top and dark jeans.

Alexis swallowed hard when she saw him. "You caught it?"

He ducked his head modestly. "I'm nowhere near the fisherman my dad is, but I got lucky that day. He was ecstatic."

"Your house is really sweet," she said, trying to focus on the interior of the house instead of the interior of his jeans.

"Thanks, but I can't take all the credit. My mom loves to decorate. She brings over her HGTV magazines and goes to town."

"Well, your mom has good taste."

"I'll tell her you said so. Can I get you a drink?" he asked, heading for the refrigerator.

"Is it too early for my medicine?" she asked, only half-joking.

"I don't have any whiskey," he said, pouring a tall glass of water. He chugged it down. Lawn mowing was thirsty work.

"Water's fine for me," she said.

He poured her a glass and brought it to the coffee table in the living room. This was the room he spent most of his time in; Alexis could see that from the stacks of spiral notebooks and the three guitars leaning against the wall.

"You still write longhand?" she queried, settling down on the couch.

He bent his head in mock shame. "I know, I know. I'm old school. I can't help it. The words seem to hold more meaning when I form each letter myself."

"You're a romantic," she said simply. "You probably wouldn't be a very good musician otherwise."

He relaxed into the couch and nodded. "I take that as a compliment."

He looked irresistible sitting there, so comfortable with himself and in his environment. She remembered the feel of his hands under her clothes and shifted in her seat.

"Should we get going?" she asked.

"How about a song before we head out?" he asked. "It's not every day I get to play for a beautiful woman right in my own living room."

"Oh, I doubt that," Alexis said. She knew plenty of women who would line up outside to have a guy like Tyler strum his strings for them.

He picked up the nearest guitar and rested it on his thigh. His fingers started moving before Alexis had a chance to make a request. He clearly had a song in mind. As Tyler began to sing, Alexis was conscious of her heart thumping inside her chest. She didn't recognize the song, but the combination of Tyler's smooth voice and chiseled features was so sexy that Alexis found herself too distracted to listen to the lyrics.

Midway through the song, Tyler lifted his blue eyes from his guitar and met Alexis's admiring gaze. He carried on singing while keeping his eyes locked on hers. Alexis began to throb in places she'd once assumed would be neglected for the rest of her life. She could see from the bulge in his jeans that the intensity of the moment was having a similar effect on Tyler. He finished the song, still fixated on her, and placed his guitar against the wall without looking away. Alexis reminded herself to breathe.

"What a beautiful song," she said, her voice catching.

"You don't know it?" he asked, clearly surprised. When she shook her head, he said, "River by Joni Mitchell. One of the all-time greats."

"I can see why."

"You're so beautiful, Alexis," he told her, sliding onto

the couch beside her. "It isn't fair to all the other girls."

"Tyler," she said by way of objection. Her flaming cheeks didn't escape his notice.

"I won't bite," Tyler said. "Unless you want me to," he added with a sly grin. Boy, did he want to. He wanted to bite and lick and nibble every inch of her.

He still smelled like freshly cut grass and Alexis resisted the temptation to caress his chest. "First blindfolds, now biting. Whatever next, Tyler Barnes?"

Tyler kissed her forehead gingerly before standing up. "Okay, have it your way. Since everything's packed and ready, we'd better go because if I sit on this couch with you one more minute, I might not be able to control myself."

Alexis exhaled deeply before lifting herself off the couch. She understood the sentiment all too well.

Verde Beach was an isolated spot on the north end of the island that was popular with fishermen. Thanks to conservation laws, the north end remained relatively unspoiled and spotting wildlife was pretty much a guarantee. Algae were commonplace in the shallow part of the water, which was how the beach originally got its name.

They towed Tyler's yellow dinghy behind the golf cart and made the twenty-minute trek to the beach.

"Are there still eagles here?" Alexis asked as they approached the beach.

"This time of year, especially. When it gets too cold up

north, they nest here. One of the most amazing sights on the island. They're partial to those tall pine trees over there," he told her, gesturing toward a cluster of trees. "I brought binoculars in case they decide to make an appearance."

Alexis was impressed with Tyler's planning. He came fully prepared with a blanket and a backpack crammed with food, bottles of water, binoculars, and a change of clothes in case they got wet.

As Tyler rolled out the dinghy and set to work, Alexis took time to admire the surroundings. Verde Beach was so different from other beaches on the island, it seemed to belong someplace else entirely.

"Shouldn't we have gone out early if we want to see fish?" she asked.

"We haven't come to see fish."

"Oh." Alexis's interest was piqued.

"Are you hungry?" he asked. "I packed plenty of food. I thought we could have a picnic on the beach."

"What's the dinghy for then?" she asked.

He gave her a sidelong glance. "Were you the kind of kid who peeked at your Christmas presents before the big day?"

"I'm sorry. I'll be good."

He cocked an eyebrow. "I didn't say I want you to be good."

She felt that familiar tingle between her legs, the one Tyler seemed to be capable of calling forth with a mere look, and fought the urge to launch herself into his arms.

She imagined herself pushing him back onto the sand and straddling him. Her blush grew deeper and she cleared her throat.

"Shall I spread the legs…I mean, blanket?" She was certain that her entire face was scarlet.

"Feel free to spread anything you like."

"We'll get a decent sunset here, I would think," she observed, changing the subject as quickly as humanly possible. She pulled the rolled up blanket from the cart and unfurled it across the sand.

"We will. We're far enough to the west of the island to get a good view."

It seemed fairly isolated. Looking around, Alexis wondered whether anyone would stumble across them if she decided to do something rash. She was so torn between holding on to Mark and reaching for Tyler with both hands. When she was with him, she felt better about herself, about everything. Her usual bravado was born out of her abilities. Tyler, however, infused her with a confidence unrelated to her intelligence or her work ethic. It was like he'd glimpsed her very essence and declared it worthy.

"You seem far away," he commented, unwrapping two sandwiches and handing one to Alexis.

"I'm getting closer," she replied with a smile. "Promise."

"Closer is a word I like to hear from your lips," he said before taking a hungry bite of his sandwich.

"Tuna?" she asked as she scrutinized the sandwich.

He nodded and swallowed. "My mom's secret recipe. I can't tell you what the special ingredient is."

"Love?" she asked, batting her eyelashes at him.

"Are you making fun of my mother?" he asked with mock indignation.

"I wouldn't dream of it. I hate to ask, though. Shouldn't these be shaped like hearts? Did your mom not love you enough to use cookie cutters on your sandwiches?"

"Now you've done it," he said, tackling her. His sandwich flew to the blanket as he began tickling her. She fell backward on the blanket, laughing so hard she couldn't keep her eyes open. That wicked laugh of hers was going to be the end of him.

"And she left the crusts on," she continued between gasps of laughter. "You were truly neglected."

"I like the crust," he insisted, as his fingers deftly amused her.

Her side began to ache from laughing so hard. "Truce," she declared.

He stopped tickling her and held up his hands in acquiescence. Watching her writhe beneath him as he tickled her had stirred up Tyler's desire, not that it was ever far from the surface. He craved her like he needed air.

"You eat," he said.

"Where are you going?" she asked.

"I want to see how cold the water is." He slipped off his shoes and walked to the water's edge. The truth was that he needed to cool off. He didn't want a painful erection to ruin the romantic evening he had planned.

He waded through the water for a minute, pretending to scout for birds, letting the winter chill of the water work its magic on his manhood. By the time he walked back to the blanket, Alexis had polished off a sandwich and a banana.

"You were really hungry," he remarked with a chuckle.

"I worked up an appetite," she said.

For a split second, he thought he caught a look of longing flash across her face and his spirits soared. He ate his sandwiches and chugged down the water, eagerly awaiting the big reveal.

"There's another sandwich, if you're still hungry. I made them small."

"I'll wait."

They sat together and admired the sunset until Tyler jumped up without warning.

"What's the emergency?" she asked.

"It's time," he announced, rolling the dinghy to the water.

"We're going in now?" she questioned him. "It's getting dark."

"That's the point."

She followed him down to the water and removed her shoes.

"You might want to roll up your pant legs," he suggested.

She complied and waded through the water to climb into the boat as Tyler held it steady. He climbed in after her and began to row them over the ripple of waves.

"Are we going far?" she asked, looking around nervously.

"No, just far enough." He rowed them out a reasonable distance and stopped.

She gave him a curious look. "Tyler, what are you up to?"

"I've always wanted to share this with someone, but I didn't want to take just anyone." He reached down and dipped his hand into the water. As he moved his hand back and forth, the water lit up beneath it.

"Tyler, that's amazing," Alexis exclaimed. She glanced back toward the beach and noticed that the waves now glowed as they rolled into shore. It was incredible. "Can I try?"

"I hoped you would."

She dragged her hand through the water and watched as it glowed. "I've never seen anything like this."

"Bioluminescence," he told her.

"It's like magic," she said in awe.

"It's the algae." He watched her lean over the boat to move both hands through the water. The movement illuminated the water around her and it looked as though she was surrounded by starlight. Somehow this seemed fitting to Tyler.

"Magic algae. Who knew?" she said, mesmerized by the beauty of it. "How did I not know about this before? Something else I ignored?"

He shook his head. "It's more recent and it's not all the

time. Seems to come and go with certain weather conditions."

"I feel like a fairy," she said.

"Watch behind the dinghy," he said and began to row. Alexis turned around and saw the wake lit up as well. "It's a chemical reaction."

"Don't spoil it with science," she said, giving him a playful swat.

"I thought I was the romantic," he teased.

"I think anyone would be a romantic out in this," she said truthfully. "How many women have you impressed with this fantastic display, Mr. Peacock?"

"I told you," he said, "I didn't want to bring just anyone."

She stared at him, drinking in his gorgeous face. His blue eyes shone even in the growing darkness. "Tyler, I don't deserve you."

"What do you mean? Why would you not deserve me?"

She sighed. "I'm not fun and romantic like you. I'm ornery and selfish and a workaholic. I don't socialize with nice humans. I'm the old woman who sits with her baseball bat and yells at kids to stay off her lawn."

"That's usually an old man." He smiled and flashed the dimple that made Alexis weak in the knees. Good thing she was sitting down.

"Sexist."

"Well, that's not the Alexis I've seen." He reached forward and took her hands in his. "I don't know where you get this image of yourself."

"Oh, I don't know, my family, my colleagues, my boss. The mirror in my room." She ticked them off on her fingers.

Slowly, he closed each finger and covered her hand again with his own. "Alexis, you're the most amazing woman I've ever known. You're beautiful, you're smart, you're funny. I know you think you deserve to wallow in sadness, but you're wrong."

They sat cloaked in darkness now, except for the light that rippled as the waves crashed against the shoreline. Even though they were in a boat in the ocean, the moment felt completely intimate to Alexis.

"It feels appropriate that I'm sitting in blackness," she whispered, "because that pretty much sums up my soul."

It pained Tyler that she felt this way. He figured the only way to convince her otherwise was to continue to show her how much he loved her.

"Alexis, you are not the darkness." He stuck his hand back in the water and swished it around until it blazed with light. "This is the light I saw in you when we were younger and it's the light I've seen in you every day since you walked back into my life. Each time I've been here over the years, admiring this miracle, has reminded me of you. That's why I brought you here tonight."

He pulled her across to him and held her tightly against his chest. Alexis closed her eyes when he began to stroke her hair.

"I don't know how long I'm going to have your

attention, Alexis. I don't know what your plans are after you leave here, but I'll tell you one thing, I don't want you to go back into the world without knowing how I feel about you, not because I want to tell you, but because I think you need to hear it. I have been in love with you since we were sixteen years old. Every woman I've been with has paled in comparison and when I dream, I dream of you. Now do you think I'm the kind of man who would waste years of his life loving a soulless, selfish shrew?"

She wanted to believe he was right, that she was a better person than she believed. He was such an amazing man. He deserved a woman who matched his passion for life and love. Could she possibly be that woman?

She became acutely aware of his biceps wrapped around her shoulders and the feel of his rock-hard abs pressed against her. Her body certainly wanted her to be that woman.

"I'm not telling you all this to put pressure on you," he said in a low voice. "I know you have your issues to work through, but…" He didn't get to finish the rest of his sentence as her lips locked onto his. He laced his fingers through her hair as she slipped her hand under his shirt to feel the ripple of his muscles.

"Alexis," he murmured, kissing the curve of her neck.

"What?" she whispered.

"We are probably safer doing this on dry land."

"I thought you were all about taking chances," she teased.

"Not this kind," he said, giving her a quick kiss before picking up the oar. As he rowed them back to shore, Alexis had another chance to admire the glowing seascape.

"Thank you, Tyler," she said. "I'll always remember this."

"That was the plan," he said.

Once they were in shallow water, she climbed out of the dinghy and waded back to the sand. Tyler pulled the boat out of the surf and rolled it back to the golf cart. Alexis made her way back to the blanket, relying on moonlight to direct her. She hadn't realized how chilly it had become. She'd been sheltered by Tyler and the boat. She felt his arms wrap around her once more and she turned into him. His finger lifted her chin toward him and she felt his lips once more. He sucked gently at her lower lip and Alexis felt pangs of lust shoot down her legs.

"I'm yours, Alexis," he said softly. "Whenever you want me, I'm yours."

She sank deeper into him, quivering as his hand snaked its way inside of her clothes. He pushed her bra up and over her breasts and gave her nipple a light squeeze between his fingers. Alexis gasped at the sensation of pleasure tinged with pain. For so long, Alexis seemed to feel only pain. For Tyler to show her that pleasure could be found alongside it, Alexis felt heartened. Maybe he was right. Maybe there was hope for her, after all.

She unzipped his pants and dropped to her knees on the blanket. Tyler had given her so much in such a short time, had loved her unconditionally for so many years. She wanted to show him her appreciation.

"Alexis, are you sure?"

She took the length of him in her hand, stoking the fire of his erection. When she gently raked her nails along his inner thigh, his abs contracted and she reveled in the effect she had on him. He groaned in anticipation as her lips swept over the tip.

"Alexis," he moaned, his fingers tangled in her hair.

When she finally took him in her mouth, his heart contracted and he could no longer think straight. In that moment, the only feeling in the world was the sensation of her sweet mouth gliding across his shaft. Desperate to keep himself in check, to prolong the pleasure, he slowed the momentum of his hips and she responded in kind. He opened his eyes to make sure she was really there and it wasn't simply another of his erotic Alexis dreams. He'd enjoyed so many of them over the years. None of those dreams compared with this moment. The feel of her luscious lips devouring his erection.

Her hands moved to grip his muscular backside and he began to pump harder, unable to keep the mounting pressure at bay anymore. She dug her nails into his skin as he erupted with the intensity of a thousand dreams of her.

When she dared to look up at him, hoping she hadn't made a complete fool of herself, his blue eyes were staring down at her in wonder. His gratified expression told her everything she wanted to know.

"Not that I'm complaining, but what did I do to deserve that?" he asked.

She stood up and raised her lips to meet his. "More than you know."

"If I keep doing whatever it is, will you keep doing that?" He engulfed her in his arms and held her tightly. "I must be in the best dream of my life."

"Then don't let me wake you." She pressed her head against his firm chest. "I want you to be happy."

"When you're with me, how could I be anything else?"

They stood like that for a few minutes, holding each other, neither willing to shatter the spell they were under until Alexis inadvertently spoiled the moment with a hungry stomach.

"Sorry," she whispered, embarrassed by her rumbling belly.

He chuckled and kissed the top of her head before releasing her. "Was my picnic not enough for you?" he asked as he zipped up his trousers.

"I guess the sandwich was small," she admitted, remembering the other tuna sandwich. She peered at the blanket. "The other one must be here somewhere."

"Alexis, you are not eating that! It's been out here for hours."

"What? It's not like it's hot outside. I'm sure the mayo is fine." She kneeled down and felt around for the sandwich in the darkness.

"Hold on," he said, making his way to the golf cart and turning on the ignition.

The light from the cart was enough to help them see. Tyler joined her at the blanket and began packing up his belongings.

"Do not eat that," he said, gesturing to the sandwich in her triumphant hand. "Let me take you to my house and feed you properly."

She narrowed her gaze, suspicious of his motives. "Only if feeding me properly isn't a euphemism for something sexual."

He snaked an arm around her waist and nuzzled her neck. "You're in charge. If you've had your fill of Cock á la Tyler, then real food it is."

She elbowed him playfully. "Was that the best dish you could come up with?"

"Hey," he said teasingly, "it's a delicacy here on the island."

"So you're saying your cock is like truffles."

Without warning, he scooped her up in his arms and carried her toward the water as she squealed in protest.

"Don't you dare, Tyler Barnes," she screamed.

"I already dared," he said, gazing into her eyes. "And I'm so glad I did."

Chapter Seventeen

Alexis sat on the edge of Owen's bed reading him a bedtime story, Roald Dahl's The Enormous Crocodile. When she got to the end where the crocodile was burnt up by the sun, Owen laughed hysterically.

"That's a silly story."

"He got what he deserved for trying to eat up those children," Alexis told him.

"Do baddies always get what they deserve?"

"No," Alexis said thoughtfully. "And sometimes goodies don't get what they deserve either."

"Why not?"

"Because the universe doesn't recognize fair from unfair. It doesn't work like that."

Owen gave her a pensive look. "I like how you talk to me."

"I have managed to lose most of my Mangrove accent. Thank you, England."

"No, I mean you answer my questions and sometimes you even use big words. Daddy tells me to go play ball. I don't like to play ball."

"Well, I think grown-ups don't like to think about some of the things you like to think about."

"Why not?"

"Because it's difficult and most people prefer easy."

"Do you think the crocodile in the story knows he's dead?"

Back to his usual thought pattern. Alexis shook her head ruefully. "I really don't know, Owen."

"But why don't you know? Mommy says you think you know everything."

Alexis smirked and ruffled Owen's hair. "You might want to steer clear of a career in the CIA." She gave him a sidelong glance. "Why do you think so much about death, anyway?"

"Don't know. I guess everything and everyone dies, right? Why not be interested in something that happens to everything and everyone? If I can understand death, then maybe I will understand everything in the whole universe."

He threw his arms open wide and accidentally smacked Alexis in the face. They both giggled. Impulsively, Alexis reached over and hugged him.

"Owen, don't ever stop questioning things, no matter how annoying your family thinks you are. Be true to yourself and you will be the happiest person you know."

She kissed him on the forehead and stood to leave.

"If I had known you all this time," he said, "I would have missed you since you've been gone."

Alexis was touched. "Me too."

"Do you think you'll stay now? I like the guy with the guitar."

"So do I."

"You should stay."

She smiled down at her nephew. "Goodnight, Owen."

Alexis turned off the light and Owen snuggled under the covers, settling happily into the darkness.

Downstairs, Betsy shook off her jacket, having just arrived home from a long day at the salon. "Hey, how'd it go?"

"No trouble at all."

"I'm sure Owen was the last one to sleep. You need to pry the book out of his hand even after he's asleep."

"Nothing wrong with enjoying to read."

Betsy tossed her keys into a dish on the counter and headed to the refrigerator.

"Please don't treat me like I'm Mom and Dad. He has books. Joe and I read to him and I love the crap out of his advanced brain, got it?"

"Glad to hear it."

Betsy immediately shifted gears. "Do you feel like grilled cheese? Joe won't be back for a few hours yet."

"Sure. I can make it."

"No, I'm happy to do it. It relaxes me."

"I like to cook, but I prefer baking. It's more precise."

Betsy proceeded to gather the bread, butter and cheese while Alexis sat on a stool at the counter.

"You should see some of my baking experiments,"

Betsy said. "Good thing I have men in this house who eat anything."

"Not all successes, huh?"

She shook her head. "Not even close, but it's fun to try. Speaking of fun, what's the latest with Tyler? Have you boned him yet?"

"Betsy!" Alexis shrieked with horror.

"Oh, sorry. You don't bone. You probably fillet or something. Much fancier."

Alexis covered her face with her hands. "I am not discussing this with you."

"At least tell me if he looks as good naked as I think he does." Betsy begged her sister with her big, brown puppy eyes. "Please."

"I have not had sex with him."

"What?" Betsy spun around, still clutching the pan. "Sister, you need to sharpen that pencil."

Alexis couldn't believe her sister was encouraging her. "First of all, it's much bigger than a pencil."

Betsy smacked her thigh. "I knew it!"

"But I haven't felt ready for...you know." Alexis bit her lip.

Color rose to Betsy's cheeks and she realized that maybe she should've held her tongue. "Listen, I'm sorry about my judgy comments from before."

"Which ones?" asked Alexis with a wry smile.

"All of them, but especially the ones about you not being married or mother material."

Alexis wasn't surprised that her mother had shared her

story about Mark and her miscarriages. She knew the women had no secrets between them.

"That's okay. You didn't know."

"It's not your fault," Betsy told her. "You know that, right? Christ, who am I asking? I'm sure you read a zillion articles on the subject."

Alexis shook her head softly, struggling for the right words. "It's hard not to feel responsible, but I'm working on it."

Betsy wanted to ease her sister's pain somehow, so she offered the only thing she had, a little understanding. "I had a miscarriage between Brian and Owen. Believe me, my life can be stressful between Joe and the kids and the salon, but I sure as hell didn't blame myself. I wanted that baby."

The pan sizzled from the heat and Alexis's mind flew to the crocodile in the story being sizzled up like a sausage. Thinking of Owen made her smile.

"Do you think you'll have any more kids?" Alexis asked.

"Hello, no," Betsy said, throwing a slice of tomato on her grilled cheese. "That ship has sailed."

"Well, you have some pretty cute sailors."

Betsy studied her sister. "If it helps any, I understood, you know, why you were unhappy here."

"Apparently because I thought I was too good for all of you."

"Oh c'mon, that was anger talking. I'm allowed to be angry that my sister ran full throttle away from her family.

How did you expect me to feel? Happy? Rejection stings."

"I guess I didn't really think you'd care. We weren't exactly close."

"No shit, but it doesn't mean it has to stay that way forever."

"I'll admit, it's been nice having a sister to talk to."

"Nice? For me, it's been awesome." Betsy flipped the sandwiches. "Nobody gets annoyed with Mom and Dad the way we do. Even Joe." She laughed, thinking about her husband's occasional frustrations with her parents. "I want a permanent bitchfest partner. Are you in?"

The sisters locked eyes and, in that moment, Alexis knew that they had reached a sisterly accord. "I'm going to be a good aunt to your boys," she promised.

"I know. Otherwise, you'd be making your own damn sandwich."

Betsy flipped over the sandwiches one more time, the pan hissed again, and Alexis was comforted by the sounds of home.

Chapter Eighteen

Alexis's alarm woke her at six. Tyler had sent her a text the night before, asking that she meet at his house bright and early the next morning. She wondered if this time he intended to take her fishing. Knowing Tyler, it was something completely unexpected. He never ceased to amaze her with his thoughtfulness and ingenuity.

She showered and dressed, choosing a simple cotton dress in emerald green that highlighted the flecks in her eyes. She closed the front door quietly on the way out, hoping not to disturb her parents. She wanted her father to get some much-needed rest.

When she arrived at his house, Tyler was perched on the front porch waiting for her. "Good morning, sunshine," he greeted her.

"No blindfolds today?" she teased.

"Maybe later," he winked. "This morning, we're hitting up Little Tuna."

"What's Little Tuna?" she asked, her face a blank.

"Your parents never took you there?" Tyler asked in

amazement. "It's an island staple."

"I'm not even sure what it is," Alexis admitted. "Seafood restaurant?"

"Better," Tyler said, his blue eyes bright with excitement. "It's the fishmonger down by the harbor."

"Oh," Alexis said. "The MacAdams are a meat and potatoes family. My dad won't eat fish."

"Yet he lives on a tropical island." Tyler shook his head. "I feel sorry for him."

"Don't bother," Alexis said. "He thinks salmon is too exotic."

Tyler pointed to the shed. "Grab a set of wheels, my lady. I am going to show you what you've been missing all these years."

Alexis walked over to the shed and cautiously opened the door. She half-expected to fight her way through cobwebs and dusty music gear.

"There's no monster in my closet," he called from the side of the house where his own bicycle rested against the exterior.

Alexis breathed a sigh of relief when she stepped inside and was met with neatly stacked boxes and a shiny red bicycle complete with a wicker basket on the handlebars.

"How perfect," she whispered to herself. She'd loved riding her bike all over the island as a child, yet she hadn't ridden one since then.

Tyler poked his head in the doorway. "All good?"

"Yes," she said, rolling the bike toward the door. Tyler took the bike by the handlebars and pulled it out of the shed in one swift movement.

"I hope red is to your liking," he said.

"Don't mind the color as long as the brakes work," she said.

Alexis could tell in a glance that the bike was in good shape and that Tyler took good care of his belongings as well as his house. She hadn't seen anything of his yet that looked unloved or unkempt and she realized how much she liked that about him.

Tyler hopped on his bike and Alexis followed suit. She worried for a moment about falling over, but as soon as she began to pedal, her childhood skills kicked in. It was, indeed, like riding a bike.

Tyler kept a steady pace, allowing Alexis time to gain confidence. By the time they reached the coastal bike path, she was beside him.

Surveying the scenery as she rode, Alexis hurtled back to her youth. She had ridden this path more times than she could remember, usually alone after a fight with Betsy or to find a quiet place on the beach to write poetry.

"I forgot how incredible this area is," Alexis breathed.

At that moment, a seagull swooped down in front of her bike and Alexis swerved to miss it, knocking into Tyler's wheel. They both managed to save themselves from falling with a solid foot on the ground.

"Your biggest threat on the island." Tyler laughed and started to pedal again.

A few minutes later they coasted into the harbor area and Alexis watched the boats bobbing up and down in the marina.

"There's my dad's boat," Tyler said, pointing to a small speedboat.

Alexis read the name painted on the side. "The Gingerbread Man?" she queried.

Tyler chuckled. "Catch him if you can."

"Cute."

Tyler bounced off his seat with finesse. Alexis couldn't help but admire his skills. There didn't seem to be a clumsy bone in his body.

She hit the brakes and skidded slightly before coming to a complete stop. She carefully dismounted, avoiding Tyler's amused gaze. They crossed to the shop together.

"Mornin' Tyler," a man called from under the awning. He wore a white apron and a blue Little Tuna baseball cap.

"How's it going, Larry?" Tyler returned the greeting.

"Coming for fresh catch?" asked Larry.

"Sure am. What's new?"

Tyler leaned his bike against the wall and then did the same with Alexis's bike.

"Got some catfish," Larry said, moving behind his shop counter. "Nice trout. Bay scallops. What'd you have in mind?"

Tyler leaned against the counter thoughtfully. "I'm trying to impress a certain lady friend," he said, pretending Alexis wasn't beside him.

"Is she fussy?" Larry asked, playing along.

"No, but she's led a sheltered culinary life."

Larry sighed deeply. "That's a damn shame." He glanced around at his offerings. "How about a shellfish ceviche? I've got the perfect sized shrimp."

Tyler rubbed his hands together. "I can already picture it. Great idea as always, Larry. I'll take the crab and bay scallops too."

Alexis wasn't familiar with the dish, but she sure liked the sound of it. "It doesn't have a cream sauce, does it?" she asked. Her stomach didn't respond well to cream sauce and she didn't want to embarrass herself at Tyler's house.

"Nope. It's spicy, just like you," Tyler said, running his hand down her spine.

Alexis felt the heat racing through her body. She was beginning to warm to the powerful effect he had on her.

Tyler paid for the items and placed the packages in Alexis's bike basket.

"Thanks a lot, Larry."

"I hope your lady friend enjoys it, whoever she is." He winked at Alexis and she smiled in return.

"How about a stroll along the harbor?" Tyler asked, pushing his bike along.

"Will the seafood keep?" she asked.

"It's early enough. Sun's not hot enough to be a problem."

They continued along the harbor in contented silence, enjoying the beautiful scenery. Alexis didn't think she'd ever felt more at peace with a person, not even Mark. As much as she loved Mark, their relationship had been completely different. Their lives had been more frenetic and, because of their busy work schedules, they sometimes went days without seeing each other. Even when they were together, their minds had often been on other matters. Although it was difficult, she recognized that it was important to acknowledge that their marriage hadn't been perfect.

At the sight of a bench, Tyler leaned his bike against the back of it. "Let's sit and admire the view before we ride back."

Alexis joined him on the bench and leaned her head on his shoulder. She pointed to a large yacht further out in the harbor.

"Wow, I don't remember seeing yachts like that here before."

"That's the Prince's Pride," Tyler said. "Caspian's yacht."

Alexis's eyes widened in recognition. "The Brit?"

"Yep."

Tyler hadn't been kidding about him; he was loaded. "It's the most beautiful thing here by far," Alexis said admiringly.

Tyler covered her hand with his. "Not from where I'm sitting."

Alexis felt goose bumps on her arms. "Tyler," she began.

He touched her chin and gently turned her head toward him before pressing his lips to hers. Alexis inched closer to him. As his tongue tangled with hers, she felt the familiar heat radiate throughout her body. Her stomach tensed as his hand slid under her shirt and she swelled with desire. He pulled her on top of him so that she straddled his lap.

"Tyler, this is a very public display of affection," she rasped as his mouth moved along the nape of her neck.

"Not too public at this hour," he whispered, his breath tickling her ear.

Alexis didn't think she could endure this very long without giving Larry an impromptu show. She leaned back and he reluctantly stopped kissing her.

"Can we continue this back at my place?" he asked, a hungry look in his eyes.

"How fast can you ride?" she asked.

Tyler leapt off the bench and practically threw Alexis over his shoulder. He grabbed his bike and hopped on. Alexis pumped the pedals furiously to keep up with him. She was desperate to get back to his house before her brain talked her out of it. She was tired of her brain with its endless loop of her guilt and failures. She wanted to give her brain a taste of the primal pleasure that Tyler promised.

Once they were back on the coastal bike path, Tyler rode until he reached one of the many coves along the shoreline.

"Why are you stopping?" Alexis called, flush with need. She followed him off the path and dropped her bike onto the sand. He moved toward her and smoothly engulfed her in his arms.

"Can't wait another minute," he said huskily. He

kissed her passionately and Alexis could feel the extent of his excitement even through the thick cotton of her dress.

"Neither can I," she whispered and slipped off her flip-flops.

Feeling the sand beneath her feet and in between her toes, she glanced down with uncertainty. Her first time with Tyler promised to be one uncomfortable ride if she succumbed now. And as much as she wanted him, she didn't want to worry about ridding herself of sand in all the wrong places.

"Ugh," Alexis said in frustration.

Tyler pulled back and gave her a quizzical look. "That's not exactly the kind of reaction I was hoping for," he said.

"I'm just annoyed with myself," she admitted. "I can't...do this here." She leaned her head against his chest. "I'm sorry."

He lightly touched her cheek. "Don't be sorry. You're right. I want this to be perfect and romantic and there's nothing romantic about rubbing your skin raw with nature's loofa."

"Sounds like you've had some experience," Alexis teased.

He gazed into her eyes and smiled faintly. "God, you're beautiful."

"Let's get back to your house before the shellfish spoils," she said.

"Yes, blame it on the shellfish. You know you want to jump me," he taunted her. "Admit it."

The moment they arrived at the house, they threw

down their bikes and Tyler hastily unlocked the door. He lifted her up and tossed her over his shoulder before barreling into the house.

"Tyler," she squealed.

"Admit it," he said again.

"I admit it," she wailed. "I want to jump you, bone you, fillet you. Whatever it takes."

He carried her straight to the bedroom where he eased her down to the floor in front of the bed. His need for her was uncontrollable. His hands moved under her dress and she moaned when she felt his fingers shift the crotch of her panties aside and slide inside of her. She was so wet with desire and it took all of Tyler's self-control not to rip off his pants and have her right then. But he wanted to make the moment last. He'd waited so many years; he wanted to feel every second of their passion and every inch of her body.

Her hand moved to the top of his pants and she unbuttoned him with ease, nibbling his earlobe as she did so. Tyler tensed as she unzipped him. Alexis worked her way down his body, trailing kisses as she went, and relieving him of his clothing in the process. As she rose to her feet, he felt her tongue hot and wet against his skin. She ran it up his thigh before shifting to his erection. His breathing hitched as she lingered there for a moment before continuing up his chest to his waiting lips.

He wanted time to worship her, but she was making it almost impossible. He pulled her dress over her head and let his eyes travel down her to where her breasts spilled out of her black, lace bra. The hunger in his eyes only intensified the throbbing between her legs. She watched as his gaze moved to her matching panties. She'd never had anyone drink her in the way Tyler did. It was intoxicating.

"This bra isn't going to unhook itself," she teased in a raspy voice, longing to feel his fingers, his tongue, any part of his body, back inside her.

Tyler had fantasized about this moment so many times over the years. Now that she was standing in front of him, wanting him as much as he wanted her, he could hardly believe it was really happening. She was more beautiful without clothes than he could've hoped for. Her brown, silky hair contrasted nicely with her milky white skin. He spied a smattering of light freckles across her chest and he couldn't wait to touch each and every one with his lips.

Tyler reached behind her and released the clasp, heat filling his eyes as he watched her breasts fall free. He let the bra drop to the floor.

"You see me, don't you, Tyler?" she whispered.

"I see you," he replied. "I've only ever seen you."

She waited for him to remove her panties before she collapsed onto the bed, pulling him down on top of her. The sensation of her writhing beneath him, desperate for his touch, was almost more than he could take. He pushed himself up onto his elbows so he could admire her naked body. Alexis MacAdams was nude in his bed, ready to give herself to him. He kept waiting to wake up, to feel a hand shaking him or an alarm buzzing. Instead, he felt only the smoothness of her skin and the desire radiating from her body.

Her breasts spilled to either side and he bent his head to taste them. His tongue circled her nipple before giving it a nip. She moaned again, pressing herself against him. Then she took the length of him in her hand and stroked.

"Alexis," he breathed.

"I want to feel you inside me," she insisted.

"Not yet," he said. "I just want to taste you a little more. Don't deprive me."

Her breasts tingled as he cupped them in his hands. He moved his head to her belly, enjoying the feeling of her squirming beneath him. He couldn't wait to hear her cry out with pleasure. All he wanted in the world was to please her.

When his mouth reached her most sensitive place, she couldn't stay still. His tongue darted in and out and she opened her thighs in response. When two of his fingers joined his tongue, she raised her hips, urging him deeper.

"Tyler, I can't take it," she said, her voice low and filled with lust.

His cock pulsed in reply, but he persevered with deep thrusts of his tongue, determined to make this memorable for her. He didn't know if he'd ever get this chance again.

"Oh my God," she cried, arching her back as an intense wave of pleasure swept her away. She ran her fingers through his thick, sandy hair, panting heavily.

"There's more where that came from," he promised. He reached into his nightstand drawer and expertly rolled on a condom.

Alexis tried not to wonder how often he'd done that maneuver. Seeing his vibrant erection in front of her effectively blocked out thoughts of his other women as desire overcame her. Eagerly, she wrapped her legs around his waist and he took the hint, slowly pushing his way inside of her. She gasped as he entered her and threw her head back, the soft pillow cushioning her. She moved her hips in time with his thrusts, her nails dragging along his backside as the sensations intensified. When he pulled out of her completely, she cried out in protest. With expert precision, he flipped her onto her front. She raised herself onto her hands and knees, angling her bottom to meet his rock hard cock. She inhaled sharply as he took her from behind, his hands gripping her hips.

"Tyler," she cried as he pumped in and out of her. Another orgasm rocked her and she tossed her head back in ecstasy, her hair spilling across her back.

At the sound of his name on her lips, crying out for him, his knees nearly buckled. As her final spasm trailed off, it only took a minute before his whole body shuddered and he joined her in blissful fulfillment.

He collapsed on top of her, spent and breathless. Slowly and seductively, she rolled over beneath him and laced her fingers through his.

"Be careful with those sexy movements," he warned her, "or I may be ready to go again sooner than you think."

"Bring it," she said, squirming just a little to tease him.

Tyler gazed at her with such intensity that Alexis nearly

erupted again. She longed to stay like this, to feel the warmth of his skin against hers as he covered her with his own bare body. She was afraid to admit it to herself because she didn't believe it possible, but she knew in her heart it was true. She was in love with Tyler. Truly and deeply in love.

"I love you, Alexis," he whispered, his words echoing her thoughts. His blue eyes remained locked on hers and her thoughts whirled.

Instead of replying in kind, she raised her lips to meet his. Although she was ready to make love again, she wasn't ready to declare it. She'd been through too much heartache. Tyler would need to wait a little longer to hear that he'd finally won her heart.

Later that night, Tyler lay in bed, reliving the glorious moment when he finally took possession of her. A small part of him had worried about whether intimacy with her would live up to the many years of dreams and fantasy, but he needn't have worried. The living, breathing Alexis was so much better than the one on the pedestal in his head. His idealistic dreams paled in comparison to the reality he now faced. Her pale skin, the smattering of freckles across her chest, her fragrant smell. She was more real than she'd ever been and he loved her for it. The thing was, he never imagined her as perfect, he only imagined her as perfect for him. And she was.

Chapter Nineteen

Tilly wiped down the counters, the last of the evening chores before she retired to her bedroom. Alexis appeared in the doorway, holding a sheet of paper.

Tilly glanced up. "What's that, dear?"

"It's a poem. It was in my box, but I didn't write it. It's not even my handwriting."

Alexis walked over and handed the paper to Tilly, who glanced at it and smiled knowingly.

"You're right. It's not one of yours. Your father wrote it."

"Dad? You're joking."

"He wrote it for you, the day you were born. Betsy has one, too."

Alexis retrieved the paper and studied the words carefully. "It's good."

"You think talent like yours just falls out of the sky?"

"Did he write anything else?"

"Not much. Only when something really moved him. He only ever shared them with me. I think he was embarrassed."

"Why would he be embarrassed? It's really good."

"You know your father."

Yes, Alexis did. "Is this for me to keep?"

"That's why it was in the box. Your father won't mind. He doesn't hold on to things. Well, most things."

Alexis considered all the possible things her mother could be suggesting — grudges, anger. Hope?

"Is Dad around? He wasn't in his chair."

"He's out front."

Alexis opened the front door to see her father deflating the blow-up Christmas lawn ornaments. He already had the large plastic ones in a pile, ready for storage. Alexis approached him tentatively from the front steps.

"Need a hand?" she asked.

"No, thanks. Been doing this so many years, I can do it in my sleep." He continued with his busy work, not really giving her his full attention.

"Maybe next year you could give the lawn decorations a break."

Greg stopped and studied her for a moment. "They're tacky as hell, aren't they?"

He didn't wait for a response. "I may not know anything, but I know that much."

They shared a small laugh that eased the tension.

"Dad, I'm sorry I cut you out of my life," Alexis blurted out.

Unable to make eye contact, Greg focused on deflating the large Santa.

"You don't have to be sorry." He stepped on Santa to squeeze the air out faster. "I know we seem like dimwit trailer trash to you, but the garbage doesn't fall far from the can."

"Is that your charming way of saying we're not so different after all?"

Greg finally cracked a real smile. "I guess it is." He handed her a stack of deflated Christmas figures. "You've got about seventeen years of chores to make up for. Here, make yourself useful."

Alexis took the stack and headed for the front door. Once she turned away from him, Greg allowed the pent-up emotion to creep into his well-worn face. If Alexis had looked, she would have seen the immense gratitude and relief reflected there.

Chapter Twenty

Tyler was heading out the door to meet Alexis at The Blue Heron when he received an urgent text from her, asking him to pick her up at the high school because her golf cart had a flat tire. He couldn't imagine what she was doing over by Wilson when she was supposed to be meeting him, but he didn't question it. Alexis needed help, so help was on the way. He grabbed a spare tire and tools from his shed and tossed them into the empty seat beside him.

By the time he arrived at the high school, Alexis was nowhere to be seen. The golf cart was parked at the bottom of the front steps and he was surprised to see the tires in perfect condition. His phone vibrated again; he glanced down at the text.

"I'm at the football field," he read aloud. Football field? What was she up to?

He walked around to the back of the school and glimpsed a lone figure seated on the bleachers. As he got closer, he broke into a huge grin. Alexis was wearing a form fitting, bright green Wilson soccer jersey and a pair of tight black shorts that left little to the imagination.

She stood up when she saw him approaching and he shook his head in amazement when he noticed the white knee socks with green stripes around the top.

"Aren't you the sexiest soccer player I've ever seen," he said appreciatively. He had a hard time keeping his eyes from roaming the length of her body.

"I drew the line at pigtails," she told him. "That would've just been creepy."

She hopped down in front of him when he reached the bleachers.

"So what is all this?" he asked.

"You told me to make new memories so I've decided to take your advice. Starting with my memories of you."

"But you don't have any memories of me from high school," he objected.

She reached up and touched his face, tracing his strong jawline with her finger. "I will now."

He leaned down and pressed his forehead gently against hers. "You have no clue what you do to me."

She ran a hand down his chest and said in a throaty voice, "I'm Alexis MacAdams and I noticed you in the stands during my game because I am neither blind nor self-absorbed. You are incredibly hot."

He played along. "I couldn't help but notice you, too. Number twenty-one, right?"

She nodded and cocked her head coyly. "Do you have a girlfriend?"

"Not yet, but I'm working on it," he said. He reached

for her, but she teasingly backed out of his reach.

"I'm not that kind of girl," she scolded him in a breathy voice.

"Don't I know it," he said, his own breathing growing more ragged. Tyler felt the heat emanating from his core. He loved the way the thin, green fabric hugged her breasts; her protruding nipples beckoned him. He ached to touch and taste every part of her.

"You seem like you could be special, though," she said in her normal voice and Tyler could tell that she meant it.

"No woman, sorry, no high school girl has a chance with me as long as you're on this earth," he told her.

He stepped toward her and enfolded her in his strong arms. She loved being held by him, fully and completely.

She stood on her toes and pressed her lips firmly to his. He reached through her hair to cradle the back of her head. He kissed her harder this time, biting her lower lip slightly as he pulled away.

"Why'd you stop?" she asked.

"To be sure I'm not dreaming," he said. "An outfit like that screams Rated X dream."

She undid the button and zip on his trousers and slipped her hand inside. "You're not dreaming."

He groaned and pulled her in again for a long, lingering kiss. A sigh of pleasure escaped her lips. She ran her other hand over his washboard abs and delighted in the smoothness of his skin.

"Tyler Barnes, will you go all the way with me?" she whispered in his ear before flicking the sensitive part of his lobe with her tongue.

She could feel his shaft harden and lengthen in her hand.

"On the bleachers?" he asked. "You really are trying to make all my high school dreams come true."

"Well, the killjoy in me is pretty sure my back can't take the discomfort of metal benches," she said, stroking him while she talked. "So I came prepared."

He followed her gaze to a spot below the bleachers where a blanket was neatly arranged with throw pillows and a bottle of wine.

"I forgot glasses so we'll have to drink out of the bottle," she said sheepishly.

"Drinking from the bottle will bring me right back to high school," he said. Before she could respond, he lifted her off the ground and carried her down the steps to their oasis under the bleachers.

She ran her tongue lightly along the crook of his neck as he walked and he made sure not to stumble. He placed her gently onto the blanket and hovered above her.

"Now I don't mean to be the killjoy, but I didn't exactly come prepared," he said.

"Reach into my shorts," she coaxed him.

"Alexis, you're going to destroy me. I don't want to touch you any more if we're going to need to stop."

She lowered her gaze. "We won't need to stop." She turned down the waistband of her shorts and he saw the condom wrapper taped to the inside.

His smile broadened. "You sexy little minx."

"And I seem to have forgotten my underpants," she said with a sultry sigh.

The ravenous look in his eyes was intoxicating. He rolled up the bottom of her top to reveal her soft curves and she worked the tight top off over her head. She watched as he admired her breasts, stroking them, and then bent down to taste them. They were fuller now than they'd been in high school, so Alexis figured he was luckier than he realized.

She clutched the back of his head, moaning with pleasure as she felt his tongue flick across her nipples, teasing them.

"The wine's a screw top," she said breathlessly, "so we don't need to worry about a corkscrew."

"Stop saying screw," he insisted. "I want to make this last."

He lifted his face to hers and kissed her again before reaching his hand down into her shorts. He removed them carefully so as not to damage the single condom they had with them. Precious cargo, he thought as he dropped the shorts carefully next to him.

She was completely naked now and he leaned on his side for a moment to admire her, running a hand along her bare skin from below her hip to the curve of her breast. When she arched her back, summoning him, he thrust his fingers inside. He watched with growing excitement as her eyes closed and she tilted her head back, welcoming his touch. She was damp with desire and it made him want her more than ever.

"More," she begged, pumping against his hand.

He pleasured her with his fingers until he felt her muscles tighten around them. She cried out, euphoric, and Tyler let out a low moan along with her. He was rock hard and ready to go. He slid his fingers out and nipped and licked his way down her torso.

"Tyler," she breathed.

"What is it?" he asked seductively, running a hand lightly down the length of her.

"I want you," she said.

His tongue teased her inner thigh. "How badly?"

Her desire was so strong now, she dispensed with the games. She gripped his arm and pulled him up toward her.

"I want to see you, too," she said, opening her eyes. "All of you."

He removed his shirt first and enjoyed watching her gaze flicker appreciatively over his torso. Then she reached down to remove the rest of his clothing. Alexis traced a finger lightly along his erection and watched his abs contract in response. She stroked him gently at first and then with growing urgency. Tyler fought through the haze of lust. He wanted to be aware of every second of this.

"Now, Tyler," she commanded. "I need you now."

He couldn't wait anymore either. He tore open the condom and thrust his way inside her before she took her next breath. She gasped as he drove in and out of her, slowly and deliberately, his hands clutching her hips. She raised her legs, trying to feel every inch of him. He lifted her ankles over his shoulders and released a guttural moan as he plunged deeper inside her. Her hips matched his rhythm and he moved faster and faster until her body shook uncontrollably. Tyler watched her face with sheer joy, memorizing her look of contentment. He wanted to bring her that kind of pleasure every day, multiple times if she required it. He wanted to give her everything. With that thought, he exploded into a million thrilling pieces.

"Tell me the truth now that you've had me twice," she said, peppering the top of his head with kisses. "Am I worth the wait?"

He caressed her bare stomach. "Without a doubt. Let's not wait that long before the next time, okay?"

"How does five minutes sound?"

"Like Heaven."

"Tyler, there's something I've been wanting to say." She drew him up to her level so that she could look into his eyes. "I am so in love with you, it hurts."

His stunned expression was quickly replaced by relief and, finally, pure happiness. He pulled her into a tight embrace and kissed her fiercely.

"You know I love you, too. I couldn't hide it even if I wanted to." He brushed a stray hair from her face. "Don't go back to London. Stay."

Stay. Alexis thought it was the best suggestion she'd heard in a long time.

Chapter Twenty-One

The shrill sound of the house phone pierced the air, jolting Alexis from her sexy daydream. These days she seemed to be having sex with Tyler even when she wasn't actually with him. Now that she'd had him, she couldn't get enough of him.

She jumped up from the couch and the magazine that she'd been pretending to read slid to the floor. When she realized that she was the only one home to answer the phone, she ran to the kitchen and plucked it from its cradle.

"MacAdams' residence," she said, slightly breathless.

"Alexis MacAdams, I'd recognize that voice anywhere," a man's voice thundered.

Alexis knew his as well. Morris, her mother's boss.

"Hello Morris. It's nice to hear your voice. My mother isn't here, though, she's at Lowry's."

"That's okay. I was calling to speak to you, my dear."

"Oh." Alexis couldn't think why. "How can I help you?"

"Would you be available to meet me at Pacho's Café in about half an hour?"

She checked her watch. "Sure."

"Great! I look forward to it." Morris hung up the phone and Alexis stared into the receiver. She had no idea why Morris would want to see her alone, but at least she only had to wait half an hour to find out.

Alexis recognized Morris instantly. Same characterful clothing, much whiter hair albeit worn in the same slicked back style. His thin lips and large gums seemed more noticeable in his golden years. Alexis remembered reading that, as some people aged, certain features became more exaggerated and she decided that Morris certainly fell into that category.

She stood to greet him as he approached the table.

"My dear, sweet Alexis," he said as he enveloped her in his paper-thin arms. Alexis worried that she'd snap him if she hugged him too hard.

"It's good to see you again, Morris." She sat down and watched uncomfortably as his bony fingers wrapped around the heavy chair and attempted to slide it out. Before she could stand to help, a waiter swooped in and pulled out the chair for him.

"Thank you, Peter," he said.

"No problem, Morris. Can I get you anything to drink?"

"Surprise me," he said with a devilish grin. "My companion Alexis will have an iced tea with a slice of lemon."

Alexis nodded in agreement, shocked that Morris would remember her beverage of choice from her teen years. She'd long dispatched of her iced tea habit since the chilly and damp English climate didn't warrant it.

"Let me look at you," Morris declared. After a moment of scrutiny, he announced, "Exactly the same."

"I was going to say the same to you."

"Hogwash," he said with a dismissive wave of his hand. "I'm an old man now and I know it. My joints do me the honor of reminding me every morning."

"My mother says you're as spry as ever."

"Liar," he said, a slow, gum-filled smile spreading across his face. "But do continue to flatter me. It keeps me young at heart, if nothing else."

"You seem to be as busy with clients as ever. People still trust you with their work."

Just then Peter stopped at the table with an iced tea and lemon for Alexis and a clear liquid on ice with a slice of lime for Morris. Alexis guessed it was a vodka tonic. She seemed to recall that Morris had a fondness for vodka.

"Let's be honest," he said and took a sip of his drink. He smacked his lips together before continuing, "Mangrove Island is hardly a hotbed of legal activity, but it's real nice, the kind of law I've had the privilege to practice. Helping local folks with their needs. Sometimes I think I'm part life coach, part lawyer."

"It does sound nice," Alexis agreed and realized with a start that she meant it. After years of inflated egos and unrealistic face time and companies with unlimited funds and the demands to match, Morris's description sounded like legal bliss. "I helped Betsy with an issue recently and it was so gratifying to see how much it meant to her personally. I never get that from my clients."

Morris eyed her carefully and Alexis was quickly reminded of his aptitude for, as her mother put it, 'sussing people out.'

"No, I imagine you wouldn't," he agreed.

She swallowed some of her iced tea.

"So how nice does it sound?" He leaned back in his chair now, still assessing her. "Nice enough to want to do it?"

"Are you offering me a job, Morris?" she asked. "Did my mother put you up to this?"

Morris wagged a finger at her. "We are not talking about your mother right now, although we'll get to the topic of one Tilly MacAdams shortly."

"I've only practiced corporate law, Morris. I don't have a clue how to do what you do. Helping Betsy was easy. It wasn't out of my comfort zone."

"Do you think I came straight here from law school and threw up a shingle? Heck no. I paid my dues in a big Miami firm before I jumped to the island."

"Really?" Alexis couldn't imagine Morris in a big firm environment. No wonder he fled for the smallest island he could find. She was surprised she'd never heard mention of it before.

"I remember very well what it's like." He took a long

sip of his drink. "I also remember very well why I left. It's not for everyone." He shrugged. "And you seem too human for that work, Alexis."

Alexis straightened. For her, that was a pretty huge compliment. "You think so?"

"Heck yes. Somebody who can write beautiful poetry like you is far too human to be a corporate lackey."

Alexis nearly spit out her iced tea all over the crisp, white tablecloth. "You remember my poetry, too?"

"Hard to forget when I've been staring at your poems in my office for the last twenty or so years."

"Excuse me?"

"Your poems. The one about streets of fire and then the one about the golden summer. I could go on, but I daresay your cheeks have gone magenta."

Instinctively, Alexis's fingertips pressed against her cheeks. "They're in your office?"

"Oh, not all of 'em. Your mother has a few favorites in picture frames. Helps keep you close by even when you're far away." He paused, drinking in her reaction. "You know, Alexis, she couldn't be prouder of you. I know your relationship isn't all it could be, but whatever your impression is of your mom, she loves you."

Alexis bit her lip. Although her relationship with her mother wasn't any of Morris's business, she knew he had good intentions, not to mention a daily front row seat. After all, her mother had been working for Morris since before Alexis was born.

"We're working on it," Alexis said. "I think we've made

some progress."

"You know how you could make even more progress?" he asked with a twinkle in his eye.

Alexis knew what he was going to say. "If I take a job with you?"

He shook his head. "I don't want to offer you a job, Alexis."

Her eyes widened. "You don't?"

"No, ma'am. I want to offer you my practice. It's high time I retire and pass the baton to a worthy lawyer."

Alexis's hand flew to her heart. "And you think I'm the right choice?"

"I know you are."

She closed her eyes for a moment, trying to process his offer. It was so unexpected. "But how do I draft a will? Don't I need to pass the Florida bar exam? I'm a member of the New York bar." Her mind was flying in a hundred different directions.

"Now don't go making a list on me. You'll remind me too much of your mother."

"Morris, have you had the practice valued?" Between her savings and Mark's life insurance and estate, Alexis had plenty of money, but she had no idea how much Morris would want for the practice.

"Lighten up, Alexis, this is Mangrove Island, remember?" To prove his point, he polished off the rest of his drink and wiped his mouth with the back of his hand. "You figure out if you're interested first and then we can talk down and dirty."

At the mention of the word 'dirty,' Alexis summoned up an image of his dingy office. "Does the lease allow the tenant to redecorate?"

"Well, I own the building so I guess I'm equipped to answer that." He pretended to think for a moment. "I'll say sure thing. Pretty it up as much as you like. I'll even kick in for the fixtures and fittings."

He threw a twenty-dollar bill onto the table and pushed his chair back with more strength than he had when he arrived. "I'm looking forward to my retirement, so you let me know as soon as possible, alright?"

"I will. Thank you for thinking of me, Morris."

"You finish your iced tea. Don't rush on my account. I can see myself out."

With a wave, he ambled out of the café with Peter rushing to hold the door open for him.

Alexis lingered over her iced tea, her brain overloaded. Her first thought wasn't about money or even her mother; it was about Tyler. She could live here and be with Tyler. She could have a different type of legal career, just as he had suggested. No more hoop-jumping, no more faceless clients. She'd be using her skills to help people right here on Mangrove Island. Her heart thumped so loudly that she was afraid the entire café could hear it.

On the way back to Rumrunner Road, Alexis stopped by her sister's to collect the salon data she'd requested. The boys were at the park with Joe so she and Betsy had the place to themselves. Betsy was in the process of cleaning up the kitchen after a baking marathon. Several cooling trays sat on the counter with various types of muffins while two loaves of pumpkin bread baked in the oven.

"I had coffee with Sandy Ventura yesterday," Betsy revealed. "Just wanted to test the waters."

"And?" Alexis leaned on the counter expectantly.

Betsy broke into a smile. "She's totally into the idea."

"That's great, Betsy. Any thoughts on location for the bakery?"

"A few places are available in Flamingo Key. I thought I'd give Sara Michaelson a call once everything's finalized on the salon end." Sara Michaelson was a realtor who grew up near them in Castaway Cove.

"I'll ask Tyler, too. He seems to know everyone and everything on the island."

"I've been coming up with potential names," Betsy said excitedly. "Bun in the Oven. Cake-tastic. Owen suggested Sweet Treats." Betsy reached across the counter and handed Alexis an envelope. "Speaking of Owen, he drew you some pictures."

"For me?" Alexis was touched. "I have some exciting news for you, too." When she told Betsy about her meeting with Morris, her sister whooped with delight.

"You're going to say yes, right?" Betsy prodded as the oven timer bleeped. As she pulled the two loaves of pumpkin bread from the oven, the delicious scent filled Alexis's nostrils.

Alexis covered her face with her hands. "I don't know. I want to."

"Then what's stopping you? You don't want to go back to London. I can tell."

"No, I don't," Alexis admitted. "I don't have a life there anymore."

"Well, you have one here, ready and waiting for you. If you say yes, I'll even let you have the first slice of bread."

Alexis threw up her hands in acquiescence. "If that bread tastes as good as it smells, you just might convince me."

When she left Betsy's, she bypassed Rumrunner Road and decided to go to Tyler's instead. Although he needed to be at work soon, she hoped to squeeze in a brief visit. If she was lucky, maybe he hadn't showered. Then she could join him. Her body grew flush with excitement, imagining the water splashing off his washboard abs.

"A special delivery?" he joked when he opened the door and saw her standing there. He held the door open for her and sneaked a kiss as she passed under his arm.

"I couldn't stay away," she said, making her way to the dining table. Even though she was bursting to mention her meeting with Morris, she knew it was best to make her decision first.

"Now you're speaking my language," he said with a sexy grin. "What's in the envelope?"

Alexis opened it to reveal one of Owen's pictures. The word 'family' was written at the top in different colors and he'd drawn his parents, his brothers, his grandparents, and Alexis. No one had a nose except Joe, probably because his real nose was on the larger size. Alexis towered over everyone else in the picture, larger than life. She also sported wings and breathed fire.

"That's a budding artist you've got there," Tyler said, peering over her shoulder.

"Yes, he is."

He wrapped his arms around her waist and nuzzled the back of her neck. "I hope our kids have a sliver of that talent."

Alexis froze. "Our kids?"

"A guy can dream, right?"

"I thought your dreams were all about hot, sweaty sex with me?"

He slipped a hand under her top and cupped her breast. "Oh, they are. But now that I have the reality of hot, sweaty sex with you, I need new dreams."

"Mr. Barnes, are you propositioning me to bear your children? Because you know I'm not in a position to make promises."

Still clutching her breast from behind, he tightened his hold on her and drew her body firmly against his. "Then let's change your position and see what happens."

"Tyler, I want to give you everything you want," she breathed as the ache between her legs grew stronger.

He felt her nipple harden as he swept his finger over it. "I know you can't promise me children," he whispered, "but can I proposition you to try as often as possible?"

She pressed her rear into his erection. "That might be a workable compromise. I'll need to speak to my client first."

He squeezed the flesh of her breast and she sucked in a breath. "I have a message for your client."

"Give it to me," she dared him, wriggling her bottom against his erection. "I'll be sure to pass it along." A wicked grin broke across her face when she heard him groan.

His mouth worked her ear to her collarbone, while his hands worked on her front. One hand toyed with her breasts and the other hand deftly unbuttoned her jeans, pulled down the zip, and reached inside her panties. She arched her back as he slid two fingers inside her and stroked her warm center. He couldn't believe how ready for him she was. Her evident desire for him made him even harder.

"Message received," she murmured.

When she attempted to turn around to kiss him, he held her firmly in place. He yanked down her jeans and panties and bent her over the table, keeping her wet with his agile fingers.

"Tyler, please," she begged, burning with lust. She wanted him like she'd never wanted anyone before. As she cried out for him to enter her, an orgasm ripped through her.

She barely had time to recover when he unfastened his trousers. She heard the tear of the condom wrapper just before he plunged inside her. She gripped the edge of the table, unaware of her strained knuckles. Her head was swimming with desire and pleasure and all the incredible emotions he produced in her. She craved his nearness, longed to feel him as deeply as her body allowed.

"Harder," she insisted. "You won't break me, Tyler. I'm strong." She felt his hands grasp her bottom and she moved her hips rapidly to keep up with his fierce pumping.

As Tyler was about to explode, he felt her body shudder as another orgasm jolted her. This time she yelled his name, unable to contain the eruption. Only when she'd finished did he let the shockwaves tear through his own body.

"Alexis," he gasped, before slumping over her back. He eased out of her and peppered her back with kisses before standing up.

She pulled up her clothes and turned to kiss him. "You're so amazing," she said. "It isn't fair to all the other guys."

"So did my message get through to your client?"

She tilted her head and gazed up at him with her bright, hazel eyes and Tyler thought if he died right then and there, he'd die the happiest man on the planet.

"Busy signal," she said. "Why don't you try again in a few minutes?"

"You saucy minx," he said teasingly, lifting her off the floor. He still hadn't pulled up his trousers, but that didn't stop her from wrapping her legs around him.

"I'm only a saucy minx for you," she said, offering him a soulful kiss. "No one else." His tongue met hers as they enjoyed the taste of one another.

Tyler knew he could never get enough of her, would never tire of feeling her body entangled with his. He finally had the woman of his dreams and there was no way he was going to let her walk out of his life. Not again. Whatever he had to do to convince her that they belonged together, he would do it with bells on.

Chapter Twenty-Two

"Morris called," Alexis's mother announced during dinner.

"Oh?" Alexis said without making eye contact. She knew her mother would be his first call. She just wasn't sure how much information he'd divulged.

"He told me that he's retiring."

Her father's head jerked up from his plate. "Morris is retiring?"

"That's what he said." Tilly looked at her daughter expectantly, but Alexis stayed mute. "Well, it's probably high time I retire, too. After all, I have grandchildren to enjoy and your father and I have enough to be comfortable."

"Is that your idea of a hint?" Greg asked his wife.

"Don't you think you've earned a break?" she replied. "A permanent one. We live on a beautiful island. We don't have a mortgage. We don't need much." She eyed him anxiously. "Don't you think it's time to enjoy our lives a bit more?"

Greg stared into his stew, as though all the answers

could be found there.

"There's plenty to do here if you don't want to travel," Alexis pointed out. "Groups to join. Year-round activities."

"Since when are you the poster child for Mangrove Island?" her father asked with great amusement. "Last time I checked, you hate it here."

"I don't really, Dad." She glanced at her mother. "So what do you think of me taking over Morris's practice?"

"What?" asked Greg with a start.

"I want you to do what's best for you," Tilly said.

"Well, as it happens, I think it would be best for me. That's why I've accepted his kind offer."

Her mother clapped her hands together. "I hoped that was it. He didn't tell me specifically, you know, but I've known him long enough to read between the lines."

"You're going to be the new Morris." Her dad let loose a low whistle.

"We're thrilled, Alexis." Tilly placed a delicate hand on her chest. "My girls are so impressive. Betsy said you're helping her branch out with her own bakery."

"She'll be my first client."

"A salon, a bakery, a law practice," her father mused. "The MacAdams family might actually gain some political clout on this island."

"That is our secret agenda," Alexis said wryly. "I'd get my own place, of course. I wouldn't want to be underfoot, especially now that you'll have more time at home. I saw a place on Juniper for sale that's a good size."

As she mentioned the house on Juniper, a vision of her London flat flashed through her mind. The home she'd shared with Mark. Another family lived there now, filling the flat with their own happy memories while all of her belongings sat in storage, in a holding pattern like her life had been these past eighteen months. Well, no more. Alexis was ready to do more than simply exist; she wanted to live.

Unable to contain her excitement any longer, Alexis took a golf cart down to The Blue Heron after dinner. She was desperate to share her news with Tyler in person and couldn't bear to wait until he finished work. Her stomach was in knots as she parked out front and made her way inside.

The bar area was relatively quiet and she spied Tyler on a stool with a guitar on his lap, a pen in his mouth, and paper in front of him. Immersed in his songwriting, she watched as he played a few chords and jotted them down.

Alexis slid a hand across his shoulders. "Play a song for me."

Tyler moved the guitar and pulled Alexis onto his lap. "You are my muse. Maybe I'll rely on osmosis for my creativity."

He kissed her passionately and she felt the rise of his excitement beneath her.

"So I have a serious question. What would you think if I stayed here and ran my own practice?"

He stopped kissing her and gripped her shoulders.

"Stay, as in live here?"

She nodded happily.

"Isn't that what I've been begging for?" he asked, engulfing her in his arms. "You don't need to ask what I think, Alexis. It'd be the smartest move you ever made."

"Morris asked me to take over his practice and I've accepted. It's a chance to shift gears and be the kind of lawyer I'd like to be."

"You'll be amazing." He nuzzled her neck. "You are amazing."

"There's a cottage over on Juniper that's for sale," she told him.

"Oh, Mrs. Kirby's house. She's moving to Tampa to be closer to her sister."

Alexis leaned back to study him. "You really do know everyone, don't you?"

He shrugged. "Local bartender, what can I say?" His brow wrinkled. "You're not thinking about buying it, are you?"

"Why?" she asked in alarm. "Does it have defects I should know about?"

"No," he said, shaking his head. "Alexis MacAdams, if you're going to live on Mangrove Island, you're going to live with me. I want to wake up next to you every morning for the rest of my life and I want the rest of my life to start right now."

She wrapped her arms around his waist and pulled him close. "I'm so happy to hear you say that."

"Guess I'll need to have a talk with old Greg

MacAdams, too."

Alexis's head snapped to attention. "Why?"

"If we're going to live together, then I need to do things properly."

Alexis clutched his shirt and peered up at him with indignation. "If you think you're going to ask my father's permission like I'm a piece of chattel, you don't know me as well as you think."

Tyler gave her a mischievous grin. "I wouldn't dream of asking permission. I was going to ask to borrow his tools to do some work on the house."

She swatted at him playfully and he took the opportunity to grab her wrist and steal another kiss.

"I knew you were never going to leave." He placed a hand over his beating heart. "I felt it the moment you walked into this place that first night."

"You did not," she insisted with a shy smile. "I didn't even remember your name at that point."

"Didn't matter. The second I saw you I knew Fate had brought you back to me, right where you belong."

"Guess I took the long way home, huh?"

He slid a hand down her side and she shivered. "Doesn't matter. You're here now and that's what counts."

She leaned her head on his shoulder. "I love you, Tyler. I really do."

"Then marry me," he said. "I want to make up for lost time."

"Marry you?" Her hazel eyes shone with happy tears. "Are you sure?"

"Alexis, I've had seventeen years to mull it over. You bet I'm sure."

"Then Tyler Barnes, I would love to marry you." She held his gorgeous face in her hands and kissed him.

"The Blue Heron is perfect for weddings or we could do it at the beach, whatever you want."

"The Blue Heron is perfect. I'll even wear white flip-flops."

"Hey everyone," Tyler called out. "Guess what? The most beautiful woman in the world has agreed to marry me."

A round of applause broke out as Tyler gave them a triumphant wave.

"We'll need a ring bearer," he said. "You think Owen's up for the job?"

Alexis nodded. "He'd probably officiate the ceremony if we let him. Joey and Brian could be ushers."

He stood up and grabbed her hands. "I'll need to call Craig. A guy needs a best man. And you'll need a maid of honor."

"Betsy, of course."

"I'll write you the most beautiful wedding song you've ever heard," he declared. "And we can get our wedding rings from Earl."

"Earl Simpkin still has his jewelry store?" she asked with surprise.

"He owes me one, too."

"Exactly how many free drinks do you give away?" she teased.

"I helped him write a love song for his wife."

"His wife? Isn't Earl like seventy years old?" She conjured up an image of Earl with his white tufts of hair sprouting in places no hair should sprout. He'd seemed old to her even in her teen years.

"His second wife, Paulette. She's a peach."

"Then Earl Simpkin Jewelry it is."

"Pack your bags, my love. I don't want to miss another second of your life."

Alexis felt overwhelmed with emotion. Tyler quickly kissed away the tears that dampened her cheeks.

"I want you to be happy," he told her.

"I am happy, Tyler. Happier than I ever thought possible." She pressed her lips to his one more time before pulling herself together. "I'll meet you at your house," she paused and smiled, "I mean our house, later tonight. There are a few things I need to do first."

She practically ran out the door; she couldn't wait to get back to him. The old golf cart, however, wasn't nearly in the hurry that she was. She decided that, as soon as she earned an income again, she would purchase a new golf cart for her parents, as well as one for herself.

Her parents were playing cards at a neighbor's house, so she went straight upstairs and unearthed her laptop. Her first email was to Hal, thanking him for all his years of support and letting him know that she would not be returning to the firm. Her second email was to the Human Resources Director, giving her formal resignation. When she hit the send button, she expected to feel a pang of regret or a sense of loss. Instead, she felt only a sense of relief. Her last email was to Mark's parents, to let them know that she was doing much better and that she planned to settle back on Mangrove Island. She knew they would be happy for her.

Next, she emptied the contents of the dresser and set to work filling her Louis Vuitton bags, those remnants of another life. When she reached the black velvet box, she didn't open it for a somber inspection like she normally would. Instead, she stuffed it between two sweaters to keep it secure during the short journey. She intended to keep the ring in honor of Mark and their marriage. She knew that Tyler was the kind of man who would understand and not feel threatened by its presence. She also packed the infant Santa suit in the hope that, if she were to get pregnant again, the third time would be the charm. The last item to stow was, for her, the most significant. The gift of hope. Ever so carefully she placed the bottle of Dom Perignon on top of her belongings. Alexis was ready to trade in the burn of her whiskey for the tickling fizz. Tonight she planned to pop the cork and celebrate her new life with Tyler.

Alexis wrote her parents a quick note and told them that she'd bring dinner to their house tomorrow and that she hoped it would be okay if Tyler joined them. She'd tell them about the engagement in person. She slung a bag over her shoulder, rolled her suitcases to the awaiting golf cart, and lifted them inside.

All the way to the bungalow, she pondered her good

fortune. Never did she imagine that she would end up back where she started, that she would grow to enjoy island life, meet an amazing man, and fall in love again. A few months ago, it didn't seem possible. She thought she deserved to be alone and miserable. Slowly wither and die. Thanks to her time on the island, she found the strength to accept her past and, in doing so, alter her future.

Alexis pulled up in front of the bungalow and studied the outside. She imagined all the happy moments still to come. Maybe a child or two, if they were lucky. Either way, she had three gorgeous nephews to dote on. Her heart surged with hope. Alexis grabbed the champagne bottle and hurried to the front door. She didn't bother to knock. Instead, she threw open the door and stepped across the threshold, into the sweet embrace of the present.

Thank you for reading *Long Way Home*! I hope you enjoyed reading about Alexis and Tyler's love story as much as I enjoyed writing it. If so, please help other readers find this book ~

1. This book is lendable, so feel free to pass it on to a friend who may enjoy it.
2. Write a review and help other people find this book.
3. Sign up for my new releases via e-mail here http://eepurl.com/Z64nv or on my website at http://nevecottrell.com/ so you can find out about the next book as soon as it's available.
4. Like my Facebook page http://facebook.com/NeveCottrell
5. Follow me on Twitter http://twitter.com/NeveCottrell